The
Secrets of
Sevenoakes

The Secrets of Sevenoakes

Mack Shelton and Dustin Reed

Published by Mack Shelton, 2022.

THE SECRETS OF SEVENOAKES

First edition. August 9, 2022.

ISBN: 979-8215114155

Written by Mack Shelton and Dustin Reed.

For Cindy, Chris, and their families. - Mack

For Amelia. - Dustin

By

Mack W. Shelton, Jr.

&

Dustin Reed

ISBN 979-8-765-58162-9

First printing in the United States of
America – July, 2022

Cover design by Diana Savu

For Cindy, Chris, and their families.

-Mack

For Amelia

-Dustin

Acknowledgements

I wish to thank three people who provided a lot of support and insight on this project: Tracy Culbertson, Elliott Gonzalez and Branson Richter. Their insights made writing this project easy and enjoyable.

Intro.

One hundred fourteen years ago –

Sevenoakes Manor -

Melvin ran from the pond holding the eighth key tightly in his hand. When he reached the entrance to the tunnel, he shoved the key in a bag that held seven other keys. He ran through the tunnel, swinging away at the darkness, not wanting to repeat the horrors he had once endured in the challenge that led him to the pond. The gargoyles were now still in stone. But he took no chance. Melvin continued to run until he was through the tunnel and back into the maze garden.

The mansion was up ahead. All he had to do was to make it through the garden, past the reflecting pool and into the Conservatory... and then on to the basement. He ran but soon forgot his way. Left, or right? He chose left and found two more paths that seemed to lead to the mansion. Instead, another wall of thick hedges. He turned around and headed back down the path and turned right. Soon, he was near the edge of the garden.

As he approached the entrance to the garden, a gate closed, barely hitting him. "What do I do?" he yelled into the night. A statue appeared; its face then turned to human form.

"You must win, that's what you do!" The statue wobbled then fell over, providing a step for Melvin to use to climb over the gate.

Once he cleared the gate, the statue disappeared.

The lights of the mansion shined brightly, showing him that the way to the reflecting pool was clear. He ran past the pool and headed to the Conservatory door. Upon reaching the door, he found it to be locked.

The glass in the door looked to be thin enough so he grabbed his bag of keys and tossed it through the center pane. The pane gave way from the weight of the bag, leaving bits of shard glass in the

Conservatory Room floor. Melvin unlocked the door and walked in, mindful of any other tricks that were waiting for him.

The harpsichord was stationary as were the chairs and other instruments. The sheet music was placed neatly on the table by the window, apparently put back in order after he had left that challenge. Nothing seemed out of place, yet an hour ago, he had left the room in a total mess. He looked around for any sign of a creature lurking in the shadows.

He picked up the bag of keys and walked, cautiously, to the main floor. Looking around, he saw nothing out of the ordinary. He quickly crept behind the grand stairs and to the basement door.

Fearing that the creatures from the mansion would be in the basement, he looked around for some sort of weapon. Finding nothing but flower vases and other statues, he tried the basement door and found that it was unlocked.

The stairs on the other side of the door were dark. He felt the walls for a light switch when two red glows at the bottom of the stairs caught his attention. As he looked down the stairs, the glows grew brighter, revealing themselves as torches. Melvin walked down the stairs to the awaiting door at the bottom. This door was also unlocked, and he went inside.

As he entered the basement, the door behind him closed and locked. More torches illuminated throughout the basement. As before, he was committed to the challenge ahead.

But what was this challenge?

Melvin walked around the basement looking for any sign of a challenge or a task he needed to perform. Casks were stored here, as with old furniture and steamer trunks. But he saw no old books, no hanging pictures, and no statues. Cockroaches scurried from one side of the floor to the other, hiding under the trunks. He looked at the walls for anything signifying a switch or lever, but only found long crawling insects climbing up the walls or back down to their lairs behind the casks.

Standing in the middle of the basement he scanned the bench tables that lined the walls around him. Aside from the trunks and casks he found little. He walked toward the far wall and found what could be the only sign of a challenge: A safe.

Around the safe were numbers painted in black and in various shapes. Single digit numbers beside sets of two and three with the subtraction sign between some of them. As Melvin looked at the numbers, he saw only rows of subtraction but no addition, no multiplying, no dividing, only subtraction.

That made little sense to him. Why would someone go to the trouble of painting subtraction equations on a wall next to a safe? As he asked the question the answer appeared in his mind. They were not mathematical equations. They were combinations for the safe!

He looked at the dial and found the numbers ranged from zero to ninety-nine. No three-digit numbers on the dial. He looked at the wall and read:

3-892-82, 6-252-78, 5-1-11, 18-27-0, 32-401-2, 80-734-21, 99-41-30, 3-192-89...

All combinations with three digits were immediately ignored. He tried the first combination, 5-1-11, and pulled the lever on the door. Nothing. He tried the next combination, and the next but found that they were useless. He then tried breaking down the three-digit numbers of 892 to 8-9-2, or leaving off the two and going with 3-19-89, but to no avail.

He knew the combination. It was something he had read earlier... He thought hard. Could it be? He tried a set from something he had read earlier during The Festival and tried that combination.

The lever made a loud clicking sound and the door opened. A yellowish light shined from inside the safe. It was the nineth key!

He pulled out the key and placed it on the table.

The shimmering light from the safe grew faint, leaving a glowing key on the table. Melvin had completed the challenge. Holding the key, Melvin smiled, put the key in the bag, and proceeded to the sub-basement.

The steps were lighted by two torches that faded into embers as he approached. A door was at the bottom of the steps and with his candle, he could barely make out the door latch. With a tug upward then toward him, the door opened.

Melvin held the candle and walked slowly through the door. It was night and there was little light from the candle, but he could see a small hallway with doors. He looked in the first room then the next, then another. Seeing no one, he continued down the hallway. A small statue appeared, pointing at a sword. Melvin nodded and picked up the sword and continued his search.

Suddenly, a suit of armor came to life and walked toward him. Melvin screamed. A small statue came to life and yelled, "The neck! Hit him in the neck! It's his weakest point!"

Melvin took his sword and struck missing the neck. He struck again and the suit of armor fell to the floor. For a moment, Melvin stood silent. He looked at the pile of armor until the familiar yellowish glow shined from the center of the pile. He bent down and picked the glowing object.

Looking at it, he proclaimed, "I now have the tenth key."

A deep, sinister-sounding voice was heard from behind, "You have all ten keys, but will you pass the final challenge?" followed by a deep, throaty laughter.

"I will pass the final challenge!" said Melvin. He poured the keys out onto the table. He poured the vial containing a solution onto the keys and watched as the seventh key vibrated and began to glow. He picked the seventh key, held it up to the blueish light and proclaimed, "I, Melvin Everette Horton, have chosen the seventh key!"

THE SECRETS OF SEVENOAKES

The flames of the torches grew in intensity casting blinding white light throughout the room.

CHAPTER ONE

Present Day –

Cumberland Boys Home –

"You gotta know your enemy if you wanna beat'em," said Timothy, a small scrawny brown-haired boy of thirteen as he leaned up against the wall.

"Yeah, I know," said Kyle, a blond-haired boy at the age of fourteen. "But how? Do you know any of his weaknesses?"

"Not exactly," Timothy said, looking at the pavement. Other boys ran past them, yelling for a ball and laughing with each other. When they passed, Timothy looked up. "He has a thing for that lady in that movie."

"Which lady in which movie?" asked Kyle.

"That one with the super monster shark," he said.

"Her?" he asked, surprised. "She's like really old."

"Maybe it's a mother thing, like a complex."

"Yeah, mother complex," Kyle said, almost laughing. "Okay, I'll use it. Now once he sees you, he's going to come after you. Don't worry. I'll be close by and when he tries anything, I'll make fun of him and get him to try to hit me."

"What if he does hit you?" asked Timothy out of concern. "He's bigger than you."

"Taller than me, but not bigger," assured Kyle. "No, once he sees I'm there, he'll come after me and I'll hit him.

Timothy thought for a moment then asked, "What if we get in trouble?"

"Mrs. Butler won't do anything if it's in self-defense. Besides, she knows he's a bully.

"Here he comes," warned Timothy. Kyle went around the corner.

The bully was tall, roughly five foot, eight inches tall with well-developed arms, all contributing to the fear in Timothy's eyes.

He saw Timothy and smiled. "Hey loser," he yelled. "Where are your dolls?"

"I don't have any dolls, Patrick," he said, quietly.

"Oh yeah? That's not what I heard. I hear you play with your dolls in your room with your friend," he said, pushing Timothy's shoulder.

"No, I don't! Now leave me alone!" yelled Timothy.

"What's the matter little doll boy? Chicken? Are you a weak little chicken?" said Patrick, shoving Timothy with each insult.

"Hey Patrick," came a voice from around the corner. Patrick looked up as Kyle rounded the corner. "I hear you have a hot thing for that old lady in that shark movie."

"You lay off her!" he yelled.

"So, it's true! You have a crush on that old lady in the monster shark movie! You're sick!"

"Shut-up!"

"You're sick and twisted and you have a mother complex for older ladies!" teased Kyle.

"I'll get you for that," yelled Patrick, almost crying as he raised his fists.

"What would that old mommy say?" he continued with his teasing.

Patrick took a swing at Kyle but missed. "What's the matter, Patty? Mommy issues?" Patrick swung again and again missed. Kyle saw his chance and punched Patrick in the nose. Patrick's hands covered his nose as tears started to form in his eyes. He felt a little blood starting to drip from his nose. "Aw, look at Patty, all crying over some old woman," continued Kyle.

"You back off!" yelled Patrick.

"*You* back off! Stop picking on Timothy," he said, "or I'll give you more of this," he said with a shake of his fist.

An older lady walked up and broke up the fight. With a few words to Kyle, she led Patrick back inside the building.

Across the street, a dapper looking man smiled. "Donaldson, I think I have found the right boy for The Festival," he said.

He walked up the steps of the Cumberland Boys Home, an old orphanage that had been in the town for over fifty years. The doors looked old with a green covering over the once copper door kick plates. The lights hanging from the ceiling were in bad need of a good cleaning and bulb replacements. Once inside he felt a slight breeze from a ceiling fan.

The office looked old, was old. The light green walls showed signs of age through cracking and chipping. The tile floor was in bad need of a good coat of wax after years of abuse from chairs scuffing them. The metal desks were equally as old and were painted light brown or gray or olive-drab green that housed computers from thirty years ago. The workers toiled away; the clatter of keyboard strokes creating an annoyance in the man's ears. He looked around then back to himself. Brushing away any small flakes of dust from his dark three-piece suit, he cleaned his red eyeglasses and waited patiently. A clerk dropped a box behind him causing him to take a fresh grip on his walking stick.

A moment later, a large, older, obese woman appeared from a door at the end of the room. She was opening a file and reading it before she stopped at her desk. She smiled and looked up.

"Mister Je Rouge, it does look like we have a boy for you. I think you two will get along so well together," she said with a hint of joy in her voice.

"Splendid, Mrs. Butler," he said as he ran his fingers around his hat. "And when may I see the boy?"

"You can see Kyle Yates in just a moment. He's doing a 'time out' for fighting. You can take him home with you as soon as your paperwork is approved," she said, "and that's," she looked up, "Bremerton Woods?"

"Yes, ma'am."

"And where exactly in Bremerton Woods, Mister Je Rouge?"

"Sevenoakes Manor."

Mrs. Butler looked up in astonishment. "Sevenoakes Manor? That's a beautiful place!" she said while closing the folder.

"Yes, Sevenoakes Manor in Bremerton Woods. And when will I be able to take custody of Kyle Yates," he asked, knowing the answer but feeling a sense of urgency rising from the pit of his stomach.

"Typically, it takes about three months, and once-"

"Three months?" he shook his head. "I'm afraid the lady of the house will require him to move in much sooner than that."

"Well, Mister Je Rouge, I can't change the laws," she said looking at her computer screen. "But tell me, why the rush? It may help expedite the process."

"Mrs. Butler," he reached into his breast pocket of his coat and pulled out a stack of bills. "I have fifty-thousand reasons that I believe this will help you expedite the process."

Mrs. Butler's eyes widened as she took the cash. "Mister Je Rouge! This will go a long way in helping the orphanage!"

"And securing custody of Kyle Yates?"

She looked at the cash then up again. "Huh? Oh yes, mister Yates. Please follow me," she said as she stood and fumbled with a set of keys in her coat pocket.

Mrs. Butler led Je Rouge out of the office and into a dark hallway of doors. Each door led to a room where the male orphans were housed. They walked midway down the hall when she stopped at room number A-22. She knocked on the door and was greeted by young boy.

"Timothy, is Kyle here?"

"No, Mrs. Butler," said the young boy. "He's in the office with Mrs. Chambers."

"Thank you, Timothy. Make sure you get your laundry from Mrs. Lindley this morning." She turned to Je Rouge. "He's thirteen. Aspiring to becoming an engineer. But Mrs. Chamber's office is just down the hall."

A moment later they had reached the double doors that led to more offices and the laundry room. Several boys were standing in groups while waiting for their laundry. Mrs. Butler led Mister Je Rouge to the office at the end of the hallway. When they reached the office, Kyle was sitting on a chair and facing the wall.

"Kyle, you have a visitor. Please come with me." The boy turned. His shoulder-length hair barely covered the fair skin of his face and he was wearing rough-looking jeans and a blue shirt. He turned to see Mrs. Butler and the stranger wearing red-colored glasses and with an ominous-looking walking stick. He had the funny feeling of uneasiness.

"Kyle, this is Mister Je Rouge. He is taking you home today. You have been adopted."

"Really?" his uneasiness turned to excitement.

"Yes, it's all taken care of. You'll be living in Bremerton Woods at the Sevenoakes Manor."

"Sevenoakes Manor?" he said with excitement.

"That's right. All you need to do is pack your belongings while Mister Je Rouge and I finish up some paperwork."

With that, they all left the office and walked toward Kyle's room, and then Mrs. Butler and Mister Je Rouge walked to her office to complete the paperwork.

"So, you're really leaving?" asked Timothy, feeling both sad and happy for Kyle.

"Yeah, I guess," Kyle replied as he took out his clothes from the dresser.

"That was fast," said Timothy. "I mean it usually takes months for someone to get adopted."

"True, I guess. But at least I'm out of here," said Kyle as he folded his pants.

"What's he like?"

"Kind'a creepy. I don't know. He seems nice but, I don't know." He put his shirts in his suitcase. "Still, I'm going to miss this place."

"I thought you wanted out of here," said Timothy.

"I do, but I'm going to miss my friends," he put his hand on Timothy's shoulder. "And I'm going to miss you."

"What else are you going to miss?"

Kyle thought for a moment as he put the pants in his suitcase. "I'm going to miss the outings, like when we all went fishing. And I'm going to miss the dance nights with the girls' home," he smiled.

"Yeah, I like those," said Timothy.

"And I'm going to miss the art show." Kyle grabbed his socks from the dresser. "I was going to make something special this year," he said as he put the socks in the suitcase. "Oh well, I guess you'll have to make it for me. And this year, you might win!"

"What were you going to make?"

"I was going to make a volcano," he said, taking his underwear from the dresser.

"That's been done," said Timothy. "Everybody wants to do those."

"Yeah, but this time I was going to make a small town at the bottom of the volcano, so when it erupts, it destroys the town!" he said with a laugh.

"That's sick!" laughed Timothy. "And you can put a doll of Patrick in the town and let him get swallowed up by the lava!"

"Yeah! I like that idea." He put the underwear in his suitcase. "Think you can build it? I mean you wanting to be an engineer and all."

"Yeah, I can build it. Just need to get all the things together and use a couple of big nine-volt batteries."

"There you go! Yeah, you'll have it built in no time." Kyle sopped packing and looked around the room, then back to Timothy. "Yeah, well, send me some pictures of it, especially of Patrick getting swallowed up by the lava."

A tear came to Timothy's eye. And then another.

Kyle saw the tears, "Don't cry, Timothy."

"I'm not, it's the dust..." he stopped knowing that Kyle wouldn't buy his lie. "Yeah, I guess it's hitting me. You've been here since you were eight and I was here since I was six, and now, you're leaving at fourteen. I've made a lot of friends here, including you. A lot of other guys are getting adopted and I've always wanted my chance to leave. Now that you're leaving, I'm starting to miss you, but I'm happy that you're finally getting adopted. But it's still hurts a little."

"Well, if you want me to stay, I could say 'no', but that would screw up more chances in the future," said Kyle.

Timothy wiped his eye. Kyle watched then looked at the floor, "I guess, if it doesn't work out, I'll be back. That's what happened to David. Had a nice place but it didn't work out. Same thing with Carl."

"Carl kept getting into fights with their son, so they sent him back."

"Oh, yeah. I remember that. Now he's in that juvenile home."

Timothy thought for a moment. "With you gone, Patrick will start bullying me again."

"I doubt that," said Kyle. "Just hit him in the nose and keep Mrs. Chambers on your side at all times."

There was a knock at the door. "Kyle, are we ready?"

"Yes, ma'am," he said as he opened the door.

"Good. Mister Je Rouge is waiting for you in the office. And you should see the nice car he has! Chauffeured here in a Rolls-Royce!"

"Rolls-Royce! Wow!" exclaimed Timothy. "He must be rich! Can't wait to see all the toys he'll give you!"

"Now, Timothy," said Mrs. Butler, "Let's not assume anything. Kyle must leave now. But perhaps Kyle can invite you over sometime."

"Yeah!" said Kyle. "I'll get settled in and see about having you over, you and the guys!"

They said their good-byes and Timothy followed Kyle and Mrs. Butler to the office. Timothy stopped at the door and looked in to see Mister Je Rouge smiling and talking to Kyle. He put his head down and turned to leave, knowing that he had lost his best friend.

As they walked outside, Mister Je Rouge pointed to the car with his walking stick. The chauffeur opened the back door then took Kyle's suitcase.

"Step inside and relax," said Mister Je Rouge. "It's going to be a long ride."

Once the chauffeur put the suitcase in the truck, he climbed in the driver's seat and soon they were on their way.

"Wow, what kind of car is this?" knowing that it was a Rolls-Royce but wanting Je Rouge to tell him.

"This is a 1907 Rolls-Royce Silver Ghost."

"So old, but I like it," Kyle said as he felt the seat.

"Old, slow, but sturdy, and of course beautiful. It's been well maintained over the years." said Je Rouge with a smile.

"Where is the house?" asked Kyle.

"The *house* is about an hour from here, near Bremerton Woods. You'll like it. Big mansion with six floors, a reflecting pool, a garden that's constructed into a maze, and a pond in the back with plenty of fish for you to catch. The kitchen staff are excellent cooks. The chef makes an exquisite steak as well as a great beef stroganoff that simply melts in your mouth." He looked at Kyle realizing the boy's age. "But perhaps you'd enjoy pizza."

"Yeah!" Kyle's eyes grew wider.

"The chef makes one that you would swear had come from Italy."

"Are there other kids there?" he asked, trying to contain his excitement.

"Kids?" Je Rouge asked, not quite sure how to answer. "There are some playmates there for you. You'll meet them tonight at dinner. First, when we arrive, you'll be shown to your room and then around the mansion. Dinner will be served precisely at seven and then I will show you the outside, the garden and pool. After that, you will retire. Breakfast will be promptly at eight. Shortly after breakfast, Festival will begin."

"Festival?"

"It's an event that takes place once every seven years in honor of the original owner of Sevenoakes Manor. There will be lots of food and music. There will also be a contest that you, being the newest member of the Manor, are obliged to participate."

"Sounds like fun!" Kyle said. "What do I have to do in the contest?"

"You will be informed at the proper time," assured Je Rouge. "Sit back and relax, young Kyle. Tell me about yourself."

"Well, I was born in Augusta, Maine. My parents both died in a plane crash when I was three..."

"Yes, young Kyle, please continue," said Je Rouge, nodding assuredly.

"I was sent to my uncle's house for a couple of years then to my grandparent's farm. I stayed there until I was eight and when they got too sick to take care of me," he paused, "I was sent to the orphanage."

"I see," Je Rouge commented with interest. "And did you participate in any sports in school?"

"I played baseball one year, track the rest of the time," he said, proudly.

"I must ask, young Kyle. Living with all those boys, did you ever engage in pugilism?"

"Engage in what?"

"Pugilism. Fisticuffs. I'm asking, did you ever get into any fights with the other boys?"

"Oh that. Mrs. Chambers and Mrs. Butler both told me that was out of my record..."

"It's quite all right. You're in no trouble. I was just curious."

Kyle looked out the window before speaking. "Yes, I was in a fight. We had a bully who picked on me and my friend, Timothy. I stood up to him and socked him in the nose."

"The bully. Was he bigger than you?" asked Je Rouge.

"Well, sort of. He was taller than me, but I still beat him. He cried but I'll bet that he will never pick on Timothy again," Kyle said, triumphantly.

"Well, looks like you've led a pretty active and interesting life," said Je Rouge. "When you get settled in at your new home there will be a lot of interesting things for you to get into." The rest of the ride was full of excited questions from Kyle and positive answers from Je Rouge.

They arrived at the Manor and hour and a half later. The car was stopped at the gate and Kyle noticed an older man signing the car in. He waved the car through and the car drove uphill on a road that was almost covered by trees. They rode over a stone bridge that had a plaque on a black pole. As Kyle tried to read the names on the plaque, Je Rouge directed his gaze to the other side of the car. Trees were lining the front bottom area of the front yard of the mansion. At the top of the hill was the mansion.

The car stopped and the chauffeur got out and opened the back door allowing Je Rouge and Kyle to climb out. He closed the door and went back to the trunk.

Kyle got out of the car and looked at the mansion. Gargoyles were placed on every corner and above the windows. The windows were arches that ended in points. The brick was old but without ivy growing on it like he had seen in old movies and in books.

"Well, Kyle, this is it. Your new home. Welcome to Sevenoakes Manor." With that, he led Kyle up the steps and to the front door. The door opened before they got to it and another older man dressed in black pants, white shirt sleeves, and a gold and black vest welcomed them in.

Kyle stepped inside and looked around. The foyer was adorned with small tables and flowers. Statues of people in various states of emotional display stood next to each table. A large grandfather clock was at the end and off to the right of the foyer. As he looked at the time, the clock chimed three times, indicated three o'clock.

To the right of the foyer was a doorway that led to a small drawing room, to the left the door was closed. Straight ahead was a large room that rose three floors high.

"This is the main ball room. When we entertain guests, we use this room. We have a small orchestra positioned here," he said, pointing to the left near the windows, "and the bar over there," he said, pointing to the right by another door and the grand staircase. "Of course, the drinks served will not be to your liking. But worry not, young Kyle, they will serve you some nice soft drinks from all over the world."

Kyle looked at the white marble floor with the dark green lines that reminded him of mint-marble ice cream. The stairs also had marble steps as well as railings. A red carpet seemed to flow down like a waterfall from the top to the floor in front of him. Je Rouge led him up the stairs with the butler in the gold and black vest following behind with Kyle's suitcase.

When they reached the top of the stairs, Kyle saw that another set of stairs led to the third floor. From there, it looked to him like the stairs turned back toward the front of the mansion and led to the upper floors. Kyle was amazed at the old house and was surprised that he had never heard much about it, except that it was a big and glorious mansion.

"I wanted you to see the stairs and the other floors, which is why we're taking the stairs. Otherwise, we'll use the elevator," he said, pointing to the right. "You can't see it from here. It's hidden in the walls. The original master of the manor felt that having an elevator was only for a select few people but also a sign of weakness and somewhat in bad taste, so he had it hidden from view," he said, leading them up the second flight of steps. Kyle noticed the ease with which Je Rouge spoke and walked up the stairs without the slightest hint of being out of breath. He turned and saw that the butler also appeared to be breathing normally.

Reaching the top of the second staircase, Je Rouge stopped and pointed to the adjoining staircases. "To the right of us, these stairs lead up to the fourth, fifth and sixth floors. Up there are the library and two laboratories. The last owner was an alchemist following in his ancestor's footsteps. He, too, was an alchemist. On the fourth floor, there is mainly extra rooms and storage. I'm sure you'll find a lot of old things stored up there. But it's clean.

"The stairs to our left leads straight up to the third floor. That floor is mainly the bedrooms when this place used to keep kids, such as yourself. Donaldson," he said, indicating the butler and chauffeur, "sees to it that the staff keeps that and all rooms on all floors clean and tidy. No spooky cobwebs, no scary creaking doors in this place," he said with an almost evil smile.

They walked toward the end of the hall but stopped one room shy of the end. "This is your room," he said as he opened the door. Kyle walked inside and looked around in amazement. The bed was bigger than the ones he and the other boys slept in back at the orphanage. A private bathroom with a shower was in the corner opposite the walk-in closet. A chandelier hung above the bed, and a writing desk stood next to the window and a small bookcase stood on the other side of the window. "Do you like it?" asked Je Rouge.

"Yes!" he said as he looked in the closet. Donaldson placed the suitcase on the bed.

"Will there be anything else, sir?" he asked in a rough English accent.

"No, Donaldson, that will be all. I think young Kyle would like to unpack and get freshened up before dinner," replied Je Rouge. He turned to Kyle, "I'll show you the grounds after dinner. Relax now, take a nap if you wish, but be dressed and ready for dinner at seven."

Kyle was now left alone in the big room. Dinner would take an hour and the sun was going down, so how did Je Rouge expect to show him the grounds, he thought. Must be well lit, he decided and resumed looking over the room. The books on the shelves were old and from authors he had never read, nor heard of. Books on philosophy, science, fantasy, and general fiction seemed to round out the previous occupant's collection of what he may have viewed as "fine reading." But Kyle thought differently of the books and went to the closet.

The door opened without the slightest hint of a creek, as Je Rouge had said. A light was on the ceiling and was operated by a pull chain. When he pulled on the chain, the room lit up revealing to him the various shelves and drawers. Now he knew why there was no chest of drawers in his room; it was in the closet. He opened his suitcase and started putting the clothes in the drawers and hanging up what shirts and pants he had. Perhaps Je Rouge could buy him a wardrobe, he thought. Soon, there was a knock at the door.

The door opened and Donaldson walked halfway inside. "Master Je Rouge thought you would be more comfortable at dinner in this outfit." He placed the outfit on the desk chair and put a pair of dress shoes on the floor at the foot of the bed. "Will there be anything else for you, sir?"

Kyle was taken back by the question. "Uh, no, no, I think I'm fine. Dinner at seven?"

"Yes, Master Kyle. Dinner at seven." And with that, Donaldson closed the door.

Kyle smiled and felt that he had to call Timothy to tell him about the mansion and his new surroundings.

"Hey Kyle," answered Timothy.

"Hey, man you should see this place! Six floors and a pond and all kinds of stuff!"

The next few minutes were spent catching up on the evening at the orphanage as well as the clothes Je Rouge had for Kyle.

"I mean, this morning I was 'orphan Kyle.' Now, this afternoon, I'm 'Master Kyle'!" he said as they laughed.

"I miss you, Kyle," said Timothy.

"I'll come see you. Maybe I can talk Mister Je Rouge into adopting you," he said.

He looked at his watch and saw that it was a quarter to six. He ended the call with Timothy and took the suit from the chair and found that it was also a complete change of clothes. The underwear, t-shirt and black socks were all brand new as well as the white shirt, black pants and jacket, and black tie. He smiled then walked to the bathroom for a shower and found freshly folded towels and an array of soaps and shampoos ready for his use. "Time for the *master* to take his royal shower," he joked as he turned on the water.

Moments later, he emerged from his room ready for dinner and to meet the others at the table. He walked down the hallway to the stairs and looked around to see if any other guests were heading his way. He saw no one and wondered if he was the only guest for dinner. Having spent years at the orphanage eating with other children and the guardian adults, he was comfortable in that situation. But the thought of eating alone, or with Je Rouge and no one else, started to make him feel uncomfortable.

When he reached the bottom of the stairs, Donaldson rounded the corner to lead him to the dining room. "You're three minutes early, Master Kyle. I'm sure that Master Je Rouge will be pleased." He opened the double doors and announced to the room, "Master Kyle," he said, slowly.

"Young Kyle, please join us," said Je Rouge as he stood at the far end of the long table. Kyle looked and saw that others were already seated. "My friends," the others stood almost at attention, "may I present to you, Kyle Yates!" he said followed by an applause from around the table. Donaldson pulled the end chair out for Kyle.

"Thank you," said Kyle, unsure of how to act. Foods were passed around and water was served in pewter goblets of ice. As the dinner progressed Kyle realized that the seven o'clock time was for him and him alone, as the others at the table were to arrive much sooner. The others at the table, he surmised, were also residents. He didn't think that the dinner was necessarily in his honor, but he was the new member of this "family."

"Do you like dinner rolls?" asked the young lady to his right as she offered a plate of rolls.

"Sure," he said, taking two rolls.

"Butter?" asked the young lady to his left.

"Of course," he smiled, taking the dish of butter. "What do you all do around here?" he asked the young ladies, only to receive a laugh from them. "Well, can you tell me about this festival thing?" Again, they laughed. Kyle smiled, "What's so funny?" but they continued to laugh.

A moment later, a cart with roast was wheeled to him by Donaldson. "Roast beef, sir?" he asked, holding up a knife and fork.

"Uh, yes, please," he said, still not used to the 'royal treatment' he was getting. Three thick slices were cut from the roast and placed on his plate. The lady to is right passed a big plate of roasted potatoes, of which he took four. He took a bite of the roast and of a potato and suddenly forgot about the questions he asked his dinner companions. Instead, he commented on how good the food tasted, and received chuckles from the two young ladies.

"You two seem very happy." And again, they chuckled. "Well, what about school?"

"What about school?" asked the one to his right.

"Do you go? Do you play sports? I know Bremerton has a great football team this year, and last year their girls track team took all kinds of awards."

"We have no time for all that," said the one to his left.

"Oh," he said. "Home schooled?" Again, they laughed.

"We've been out of school for a while," said the one to his left.

"What? How can that be? You're not much older than me," he said, and as on cue, they laughed again.

Seeing that he would never get any answers from his dinner companions, Kyle focused on the food. A second round of potatoes, vegetables, and the roast beef made its way to him and he indulged as the other residents did in more food.

Soon, desert was offered. The desert cart was full of a variety of cakes, apple, and cherry pies, and three flavors of ice cream: vanilla, chocolate, and strawberry, complete with the chocolate, caramel and marshmallow sauces, sprinkles, and crushed nuts. Kyle opted for the apple pie and vanilla ice cream.

When dinner was over, Je Rouge lit a long, thick cigar. The rest of the dinner companions continued to look at their new resident then began to welcome Kyle to their home, and he was feeling more at ease. This was nothing like the orphanage where he felt he was thrusted onto the other kids. In fact, no one spoke to him for three days, other than Mrs. Butler and Mrs. Chambers, the lady who did the laundry, Mrs. Lindley.

"Well, young Kyle. How did you like the roast beef?" asked Je rouge through a thick cloud of smoke. "Not too well done, was it?"

"No, sir. It was really good!"

"I'm pleased. Well," he stood, "time to see the rest of the place before it gets too late."

They left the dining room and headed to the Conservatory which led to another alcove and to the rear double doors. Lights were on everywhere giving the impression of daylight. Je Rouge flipped several switches and the lights in the garden came on. "Shall we?" Je Rouge said as he opened the doors.

The patio was of stone with stone quarter walls and a stone fire pit in the middle. Kyle thought that the fire pit was an alter from some horror story he had read by the way the pit was shaped. Steps led to the yard with its lush, green grass. Trees were in the distance, but two rows of Italian Cypress trees lined either side of a rectangular pool of water.

"The garden is on the other side of the pool. Come," said Je Rouge, leading the way. "The pool is about three feet deep from one end to the other. It's not for swimming, but more for admiring the ducks and geese."

They walked to the edge of the pool and Je Rouge pointed to an arch that was made from a hedge. "Through there is the maze garden. Go in, it's a maze. You can walk around looking for the other end or sit in one of the benches and come back out. Once you learn the maze it's easy to go through to the other side."

"And what's on the other side?" asked Kyle.

"This maze leads to a tunnel. Through that tunnel and you'll end up at the pond. Lots of trees and other flora there. The pond has fish and other wildlife there. We go there on some Sundays," Je Rouge said with a smile. He looked at his pocket watch. "Well now, it's getting late young Kyle. I'm sure that you will want to go back and maybe turn in. Afterall, tomorrow is going to be a big day for you!"

They turned back toward the mansion and soon were back inside in the Conservatory. Kyle was amazed at the instruments that were set up around a center piece that looked to him like a piano. "Wow, I've never seen a golden piano before," exclaimed Kyle.

"That's a harpsichord, but it's not gold. That is gold-leaf on European tulip poplar. Inside is an assortment of oak, maple, walnut, and spruce. It's well over one-hundred years old, and best of all," he said, "it still plays as clear and crisp as the day it was made." Je Rouge played a few notes. "See?"

Kyle looked around, "There's a lot of instruments in here, violin, cello, all those brass instruments," he observed.

"Yes, they come in and play each evening. That's why the instruments are always out of their cases." Je Rouge stood by the instruments. "Do you play?"

"I was taught the piano, once. Wanted to play the guitar but never did."

"Well, you will have plenty of time to learn music on any of these instruments," Je Rouge promised. "And perhaps we can get you a nice guitar."

As they left the Conservatory, Kyle asked, "Uh, where is everybody?"

"What do you mean?"

"From dinner. There seemed to be a lot of people and after dinner, no one is around."

"They all do their own things," assured Je Rouge. "The two young ladies you sat with are up in their rooms working on some sweaters for the boys sitting at the middle of the table. Those boys are studying as I'm sure the rest are or should be."

"Oh," he thought for a moment. "When do I attend school?"

"That will come soon enough," said Je Rouge. "But for now, just enjoy yourself. I've seen your school record. Between all A's and B's. Not bad, not bad at all, young Kyle."

"I remember missing a lot of school when I was younger, and the truant officer showed up and I was in trouble."

"I'm sure nothing like that will happen to you, young Kyle."

They reached the grand stairs and Je Rouge stopped. "Well, I believe it's time for bed. Remember your room?"

"Yes," Kyle said.

"All right, then. I'll expect you for breakfast right at eight in the morning." With that, Je Rouge turned and left Kyle to climb the stairs himself.

When Kyle reached the top of the stairs, he decided to look around. The third floor was quiet. There were lights in the hallway but none coming from under the doors. Maybe they were on the fourth floor, he thought as he climbed back up. But when he reached the fourth floor, he was greeted with the same style of lights and a single door. No lights from underneath and no noises were heard.

He tried one of the doors, but it was locked. Everyone must be further upstairs, he thought again, but decided to just go to his room. Kyle headed back to his bedroom. He was thinking of Timothy and how he would like living in Sevenoakes Manor.

When he got to his room, he noticed more clothes were placed on his bed and across his chair. He hung up the suit and put the underwear and socks in the closet drawers. When he was done, he pulled out his cell phone and called Timothy. "Hello, Kyle?" he answered.

"Yes, man this place is great!"

"How is it?"

"Big! Huge! It's like living in a museum only without the weird artwork," he exclaimed. "I think you'd love it here. I'm going to tell this Je Rouge guy to adopt you!"

"Yeah! Think he'll do it?"

"He could, he's got the money for it. They keep giving me clothes to wear when we eat!"

"Tell me about the place." Kyle spent the next few minutes telling Timothy about the mansion, the grounds, and the first-class dinner that was served. He also told him about the people at the table and Donaldson, the butler. "Sounds great! Count me in!"

They spoke for several more minutes before Timothy told Kyle that Mrs. Butler had announced that it was time for the Cumberland children to get ready for bed. They hung up and Kyle got ready for bed. This night would be his first night in the mansion and he was both excited and scared that he would be sleeping alone.

CHAPTER TWO
FESTIVAL AND THE FIRST KEY

The morning light was peering in through the window onto Kyle's face as he rolled away trying to return to sleep. As soon as he did, there was a knock at the door, followed by the deep and raspy familiar voice of Donaldson. "Master Kyle, it is now seven-thirty. Time for you to rise and dress for breakfast. Breakfast will be precisely at eight o'clock." And with that, Donaldson left the door.

Kyle rose out of bed and headed for the bathroom and his morning shower. He already had his clothes ready for breakfast so all he had to do was dry off and dress. The water was nice and warm, like the night before, but unlike the showers at Cumberland. Those were either too hot or too cold. The mansion showers were just right. He still had his supply of soaps and shampoos and this time he chose the green ones, thinking that tonight he would choose the blue ones.

He remembered that today was The Festival and he started to wonder about that. He had been to the Cumberland County Fair the previous summer on a field trip with the other boys and that was fun. Once dressed, he looked out the window but didn't see any rides, tents, tables, or anything resembling the fair. Instead, he saw the grass and trees in the back yard as well as the pool and Maze Garden.

He left his room and headed toward the stairs and down to the dining room. Again, he saw no one heading that way. No servants, no maids, no other children, just him and him alone heading toward the first floor.

When he reached the bottom of the stairs and looked out over the Ball Room, he could see Donaldson standing by the Dining Room door with his arms down by his side. As he approached, Donaldson opened the door. And when Kyle was at the door, Donaldson announced him. "Ladies and gentlemen, Master Kyle Yates."

Those at the table applauded Kyle and he took the same chair as he had the night before, at the end, opposite of Je Rouge.

Platters of fried eggs, pancakes, biscuits, bacon, ham, and sausage links and patties were passed his way. Kyle took what he wanted and continued to pass the rest to his right. The same two girls from the night before were there, smiling at him.

"Good morning," he said, getting a laugh from them. "Sleep well?" Again, they laughed. "Yeah, me too."

He continued to eat and tried to listen in on the conversations the others were having at the table. He could make out a few words here and there about the trees, garden, weather in general, and something about "the last time." As he tried to listen, the girl to his right offered Kyle a small plate of butter. "Oh, thank you," he said as he took the plate. He took a couple of pads of the butter and passed the plate to the girl on his left. She smiled and offered him a pitcher of orange juice. He took the juice, filled his glass, then passed it to his right. When he thought he had everything he wanted, he started listening to the conversations again, only to be interrupted by a plate of pancakes.

The girls continued to look and smile, even laugh. The rest of the people continued their conversations without looking at him. He finished most of his breakfast, saving the pancakes for last, and looked around. Others were finishing up their breakfast and sitting back engaged in conversation.

After breakfast, Je Rouge smiled and lit a cigar. "That was a wonderful breakfast," he said as the smoke rolled up beside his face. "Today will be a great day, young Kyle," he said. The others at the table giggled and made comments Kyle couldn't quite understand. "Today is Festival. And beyond the doors behind you, they are setting up in the Ball Room."

Kyle gave a cursory glance then returned to his pancakes. He heard nothing from the Ball Room as the chatter at the table seemed loud enough to drown out sounds from the other rooms. But Kyle was getting a funny feeling at the way Je Rouge and the others at the table were looking at him. The smiling was one thing, but the side glances at him then the conversation with each other across the table then back at Kyle was getting annoying.

Kyle decided to break the tension. "So, what is this festival all about? Are there games and stuff like at a carnival?"

"Of sorts," said Je Rouge. "But when you've finished your breakfast," he said with a smile, "we shall go to the next room, and begin."

Kyle finished his pancakes, wiped his mouth, and announced that he was done. The others at the table applauded and left the table in a child-like excitement. "Must be a great festival," he said to Je Rouge.

"Quite the festival," he replied, smiling. Je Rouge left his end of the table and headed for the double doors. "Patience everyone. I'll open the doors, and everyone take their places. Kyle, you will enter last with me."

"Okay," he said, feeling the excitement building.

Je Rouge opened the doors, and the others ran out. When the last person was out of the dining room, he smiled at Kyle and allowed him to walk out in front to the Ball Room.

"My friends, this is young Kyle. He will be the host of today's Festival." This announcement was followed by a round of applause. "Today will be filled with splendor and fun. If the Manor Guards will do the honors?" he said, nodding toward Kyle. "Go with these men. You're in good hands now."

Two servants walked up to Kyle and led him to a chair in the center of the Ball Room floor. One man motioned for Kyle to sit while the other pulled out belts.

"What, are you going to strap me into the chair?" he asked, feeling concerned for his well-being. The man smiled and nodded. Kyle sat in the chair as the men strapped him in. When they were done, they walked back to join the crowd.

Suddenly, the chair lifted and started to slowly spin. As it rose, the crowd applauded. The chair turned five times before reaching the top.

When the chair did reach the top and stopped spinning, Kyle was in front of Donaldson, who was standing behind a podium.

Donaldson spoke in a vocal inflection that reminded Kyle of a judge he saw on an old television show. "We are gathered here this morning, to witness this young man, Kyle Edward Yates, meet the challenges that lay before him. These challenges are an integral part of the ceremony we have called 'The Festival.'

"From days of Lord Elwin Chadwick, the founding father of Sevenoakes Manor, the Festival has taken place every seven years. We have enjoyed the celebrations. We have enjoyed the music. We have witnessed a young challenger go up against the quests and challenges that await him.

"All have participated, all have failed, save one. That young challenger, who, one hundred-fourteen years ago, won The Festival and allowed those before you to leave the Manor, and to return to their time, and to their lives.

"What you, Kyle, do not know and must now be told is that all challenges must be concluded within the next twenty-four hours. If you succeed, you will be free and those of us may return to our times and our lives.

"You will start on the sixth floor of this mansion and find the answers to the challenges before you. Once you complete that challenge, you shall proceed to the fifth floor, and on down until you reach the first floor. There, you shall proceed to the garden and then to the pond. From there, you shall resume your search in the basement and then to the sub-basement. But you must successfully complete each challenge before proceeding to the next.

"Once you successfully complete a challenge, you will receive a key. There are ten keys to be found. Once you find all the keys, you will go to the sub-basement and select the correct key by using a potion that you will have to mix, one that will help you pick out the correct key, a key that will release all within the manor.

"Failure to complete just one of these challenges, or should you make the incorrect choice, shall doom you and all those who reside in the manor until such time that a challenger proves to be successful.

"Are there any questions from the challenger?"

The crowd below murmured, waiting for Kyle to give his answer.

"Just so I know, I beat ten challenges, get ten keys, use some potion that I have to make, and choose the right key that will release everybody?" he asked, almost arrogantly. "Is that it?"

"That is correct, Kyle," said the judge.

With that, Donaldson dismissed Kyle and the chair descended back to the floor. Kyle was released and led to the elevator.

Kyle smiled as he got to hear Donaldson speak more than a few words telling him about his clothes and being presented to a room full of people during meals. He smiled at his voice.

Once all three were in the elevator, Kyle looked at the servant to his right, who began to speak. "Master Kyle," said the servant, "You will start on the sixth floor and work your way down," he said, repeating the judge's rules. He closed the elevator gate and pulled the old-style lever, and the elevator came to life and began to rise upward. They watched the floor numbers flash on then off followed by the sound of a bell until they came to the one marked 6.

The servant opened the gate and showed Kyle the way out. "Good luck, Master Kyle. We're all with you." And with that, the gate was closed, and the elevator went back down to the first floor.

Kyle stood in the hallway of the sixth floor. The lights spaced intermittently between the doors did little to produce enough light for him to see. The first challenge was to be on the sixth floor, but he didn't know where. He walked, passing closed door after closed door, trying each doorknob until he found one that wasn't locked.

"This is easy," he said to himself. "They keep the room with the secret open for me."

He opened the door and found the room to be the library. Shelves of books stood higher than he had ever seen in the library at the orphanage. Globes depicting old Earth were on tables with a big floor globe in the center between four tables. Rolling ladders were placed on each bookshelf for access to the upper books.

"Now, what do I look for in here?" asked Kyle. He sat at one of the tables and took in how many books were in the library.

"Sit not if you wish to succeed," said a voice from behind. Kyle turned and jumped up from his chair as he found a small three-foot statue looking at him. Suddenly, the statue turned a blueish white and started to shimmer and come to life. "Sit not if you wish to succeed. The path to knowledge is at your tips. Climb the ladder to be freed. Ignore my advice, silence your lips, and forever in the mansion you'll be."

"Who-who are you?" asked Kyle. "*What* are you?"

"I am Enov, I am your guide. My wife, Gilda, will help your stride. My advice is golden, take it whole. Listen to me, protect your soul." With that, the little man returned to stone.

Kyle looked at the stone statue then at the rolling ladders on the bookcases. When he looked back at the statue it was gone. "Hey, where are you? I still have questions?" But there was no reply.

A million books, Kyle thought, and they all must be searched through and read before the end of The Festival. There was no way he could go through every single book. Maybe a diary or journal would help. He checked the shelves that were within his reach before thinking about either of the ladders. Why write a journal just to keep it up high, near the ceiling? He asked himself.

He circled the library and browsed for anything that looked like an old journal or an old folder, anything but an actual book. As he reached the end of the first row, he found a table at the end and near a wall. That table had an open book on it, and the page showing was of Sevenoakes Manor. He looked at it and found it to be the history of the manor.

He picked up the book from the table and carried it to his chair. Perhaps there would be something in this book that would help him with the ingredients list for the potion, and the challenges ahead. The book was hand-written with pictures all telling the story in one-hundred pages.

The manor was started back in 1791 by Lord Elwin Chadwick, born August 1759 – died February 1826, an exporter who made his living exporting raw materials to England, France, Spain, and throughout the Caribbean islands. He built Sevenoakes based on a mansion of similar design in England where he was born.

Lord Elwin never married but kept his sister and her family, and brother and his family, in the manor while he worked in his business. He courted a younger woman named Sophia McCormack until she died of consumption in 1809. Since that time, no record was found of Lord Elwin ever having courted nor seeing any other woman.

His sister, Myrtle Chadwick-Douglas, born May 1784 – died February 1826, married a young lawyer named Tobias Douglas, born March 1783 – died February 1826. They had one daughter named Amelia, born January 1814 -, during the War of 1812. She lived at the manor until her disappearance in 1828 during The Festival.

Lord Elwin had two younger brothers. One was Steven Chadwick, born March 1777 – died February 1826. He was a lawyer who worked for Elwin and his company. He married Elizabeth Maynard, born 1782 – died February 1826, and had one son named Simon, born July 1812, at the beginning of the War of 1812. He excelled in reading and writing and had keen interests in the exporting business by the age of thirteen.

The others of Elwin's younger brothers, Louis Chadwick, born June 1780 – died October 1821, was Elwin's assistant in the business, and spent many weeks travelling to the various east coast ports. He married Gladys Brock, born June 1790 – died February 1826, and had two daughters, Stephanie, born March 1816 – died February 1819, and Mary, born October 1817 – died 1891. Stephanie died at the age of 3 from tuberculosis. Mary grew up to become a nurse, having left the manor to work at a hospital in the city of Goliath Park.

Interesting information, but Kyle was no closer to finding out anything about a potion or a list of its ingredients. As he read further, he found out the history of the manor, the cost of construction, the years it took to complete, and the business history.

But then it struck Kyle. Everyone listed in the family had a birth year and the year they died, except Simon. Something missed, he thought. Even Amelia had a birth year and a year she disappeared, though not a cause of death. Simon's year of death was missing.

Lord Elwin eventually sold the business and retired at the age of seventy, and after his brother, Louis, had died. In retirement, Lord Elwin took up alchemy and practiced in the art of early chemistry and some black magic. The family story was that Elwin was trying to bring back his brother and Sophia McCormack from the dead. He dabbled in many things and tried once to market a new medicine that would help loved ones see the dearly departed. This caused a stir in the city and Lord Elwin was initially labeled a "scoundrel" for trying to take advantage of those suffering. However, Steven and their friends came to his aid and bought newspaper advertisements to sell another elixir Elwin had developed. This elixir proved beneficial in the medical community as it helped with pain from various ailments. Soon, Lord Elwin's reputation was repaired, and he went on to make and sell the elixir to local doctors and the hospitals.

Lord Elwin also opened up Sevenoakes to the local citizens to prove that he was sane and safe. He held a festival for the local children.

Pony rides, contests, performers of all sorts, and foods were the highlights of the festivals. He continued these festivals until his death.

The family story of Lord Elwin's demise seemed to be confusing and contradictory to Kyle. One version is that Lord Elwin was trying one of his creations and died from poisoning. Another version said that Lord Elwin was murdered by poison while working in his laboratory. One thing that seemed to be true was that "an associate" was to blame.

The deaths of family members, Myrtle and Tobias, was listed as a carriage accident. A horse started to run wild and tipping the carriage over a bridge. The two were found dead and had apparently died instantly.

Gladys Brock-Chadwick also died in February 1826. Her death was attributed to a heart attack. After her husband, Louis, had passed away, it was said that she was on a decline of health and "died of a broken heart."

Kyle looked at the dates and wondered how so many could have died at around the same time. It seemed that when Louis died, Lord Elwin went quietly nuts and started messing around with chemicals, Kyle thought. When he died, shortly afterward, his daughter and son-in-law died, all three in February 1826, just days apart from each other.

Kyle looked further into the book but little else was written, other than the reopening of the manor to the local population. The manor soon became an attraction and people from all over would travel just to spend the night in luxury. From the book, this lasted for about twelve years until the manor was closed off for good, citing "lack of funds."

Rumors started that the manor would be sold off to local developers. However, Simon insisted that the manor would stay with the family. He, too, became an exporter working for his father's competitor.

Not much else was written about Sevenoakes or anyone else, only to state that improvements had been done here and there over the years. No other mentions of family members or even visitors.

Kyle closed the book and wondered about his host, Je Rouge.

A moment later, he was back at the challenge of finding the journal that contained the potion. He did remember Enov saying that he needed to climb a ladder and look upward. He chose the nearest ladder and climbed.

The bookcase was twenty shelves high. Books with titles printed in gold lettering, some in black on canvas-colored covers, green, all sorts of designs, but these were printed from a company. He had to find a hand-written journal.

He pushed the ladder to his right and ended up at another bookcase and more of the same books. He looked up and down, but all the books were like the last. He was reminded of the old set of encyclopedias he used to read at the orphanage.

When he completed the row of books he went to the other side of the library and climbed that ladder. The sunlight shined into the room, striking the brass ornaments on top of the bookcases. As Kyle climbed, he could feel the warmth through his black dinner jacket. A bead of sweat had started to roll down his back giving him a slight tickling sensation.

"I'm getting rid of this monkey suit as soon as I find the journal," Kyle promised himself. He continued to look but like with the other row of bookcases, these were the same. He pulled himself to the last bookcase and stopped. The sun was still shining in through the windows, but he was in an area where the sun wasn't shining. He looked around and saw the brass ornaments shining like golden light bulbs. Twenty-four on the other side of the library, and twenty-four on his side. All shining, that is, except one. One brass ornament appeared dull.

Kyle climbed down the ladder and walked to the middle of the floor. Looking up, he saw all forty-eight brass ornaments, all shining, all but one. Could that be the answer?

He took off his jacket and tie and left them on a table as he climbed the first ladder. When he reached the top, he felt the dullish-looking ornament and found it to be painted metal. The finish was old as though it had been painted prior to being installed.

He looked at the ornament closely. There appeared to be a separation from the ornament and the wall it was supposed to be attached to. He felt it, tried turning it but nothing happened. He tried pulling it and felt it give way. The ornament came out about four inches with a series of clicks.

Below, Kyle felt the ladder shake. He quickly climbed down and saw as the two middle bookcases came forward then split apart. A wall behind the bookcases opened, revealing a small closet-like room and a pedestal with a book on it.

Kyle slowly walked to the pedestal and looked at the book. It was not like the others. It was like the family history book, all hand-written in a leather-bond cover. He opened it and found several hand-drawn pictures and hand-written notes about different chemicals. He found a table of measurements and the periodic table of elements. Along with these was a chart of the phases of the moon and predictions of the solar and lunar eclipses for the next three hundred years.

Taking the book to a table, he looked through the pages. Lord Elwin had written notes on the different formulae he had concocted and the various results. Pictures of plants and leaves were in the center of the journal with their different names: common names, and Latin names.

The formulas were not in any order that Kyle could see. Perhaps written as he made them, he thought. He thumbed through the pages to see if any potion seemed relative to his challenges.

One was for growing flowers, one was for improving paints for home, one other formula was for the improvement of burning firewood, and still another was for helping accentuate flavors of European cuisines. He discounted any of these as being no help to him. He found one that was a formula for Berignese 1135. This had to be the one, he thought.

"These ingredients seemed like something a mad scientist would have in his personal laboratory," said Kyle to himself. He tried to make out the handwriting and read what he could out loud...

Formula for Berignese - 1135

1. **Essence of Newberry – ¼ strength**
2. **Powder of Ferrous Oxide – ½ once**
3. **Illuminating bioluminescence of Lampyridae – 12**
4. **Piterenneli 837, 1/8 once**
5. **Glycerin 134-n, 3/8 cup**
6. **Petals of: Lilac (2), Daisy (2), Ivy (4), Ragweed (9), Queen Ann's Lace (3), Rhubarb (8)**
7. **Tungsten (Wolfram) shavings – ½ cup**
8. **Tri-lydaremocous – 1 teaspoon**
9. **Fermicycline Dioxide 35 – ¼ mg.**
10. **Saswyb Chlorathiesen Caporal 9 - .8 mg.**
11. **Small etched looking glass**

"What is all this?" asked Kyle. "I can't even pronounce half this stuff!"

"That's what he wrote, that's what he made. Hurry and find the ingredients, shine in the sun, die in the shade."

Kyle looked at Enov. "What?" he asked, doubtfully.

"All right, maybe not die in the shade, but your freedom will be stayed. Better?" and with that, Enov turned back into stone.

Kyle read the directions of the formula:

Capture the light of the Lampyridae with the mirror coated in Essence of Newberry. Their bioluminescence will be captured in the Newberry.

Add the liquid ingredients of Glycerin 134-n, Piterenneli 837, Illuminating bioluminescence of Lampyridae in Essence of Newberry, Tri-lydaremocous and mix together for precisely two minutes.

Add the dry ingredients as follows: Tungsten shavings, Ferrous Oxide, and Fermicycline Dioxide 35, heating to 325 degrees F. Once these have become heated, add in the liquid ingredients.

When the mixture is steady, crush the flower petals and add to this mixture. Stir repeatedly for four minutes.

Add the Saswyb Chlorathiesen Caporal 9. This must be done last!

When all the ingredients are mixed, increase the heat to 500 degrees F. This will liquify the potion.

Remove from heat and let cool. Once cooled, transfer into vial.

To use: pour potion onto keys to find the correct one.

"Enov, if you're still around," said Kyle, feeling angered, "I've never had chemistry in school. I have no idea what all this stuff is. Where do I find Essence of Newberry? What's a Newberry? And what is this Tri, Tri-lydacyclelous thing?" But there was no response. "Enov! You're supposed to guide me!"

Kyle looked around the library for Enov. After he was sure Enov had left him, he looked at the list of ingredients again. They were in the journal and taking the journal out of the library would prove problematic should he encounter something more sinister than a hidden switch. He found some paper and a pencil and copied the list and directions for the potion, folded up the paper and stuffed it in his pocket. He returned the journal back to the pedestal and watched as the bookcase closed, hiding the small room.

But then he thought differently of the family book. He figured that Lord Elwin had secrets in the book that he hadn't gotten to, yet. He also thought of what Timothy had told him about Patrick, *"You gotta know your enemy if you wanna beat'em."* That meant keeping the family journal with him, and maybe finding out some things about Simon and the rest of his family.

To his right came a rumble followed by the tinkling sound of something small and metallic. He turned to see a glowing key on the marble floor. As he approached the key, the glow faded. He picked up the key and smiled. The first key.

Only nine more to go plus finding everything on the list. The next challenge would be one floor down in the laboratories. But he had the first key.

CHAPTER THREE
THE SECOND KEY

The door was unlocked when he opened it. He walked into the room and saw that it was one of the alchemy labs Je Rouge spoke about. Tables with test tubes, bottles of unmarked chemicals, beakers, single-eye microscopes, kerosene lamps, electric lamps, and other things were displayed neatly around the lab; everything Lord Elwin had used while making his potions. As he walked around, he caught something moving out of the corner of his eye. He turned but whatever it was wasn't there.

He continued to look over the lab and wondered what he was supposed to find in there besides the key. He tried the drawers but found everything but a key. A desk was at the right of the window and situated so that the occupant would have sufficient light from the window. He tried the desk drawers and all but one opened. The unopen drawer was locked. Could this be a clue? Could the key be in this drawer? Kyle thought about it but realized that finding the first key in that one and only locked drawer would be far too easy. Still, he decided to open the drawer.

Looking around the desk for a key or anything else that would open the drawer, he found a screwdriver. He picked it up and pushed it in the space between the desktop and the drawer and wiggled it. A sound from his right caused him to look up. A small statue made him jump.

"Not there," said the statue. "Clear the dust, open if you must, but that which you are looking for is not in that drawer."

"Enov?" he said, surprised.

The statue came to life. "What you're looking for is not in that drawer," he said.

Kyle was shocked by Enov's presence. "How did you get here?"

"I started to walk. I used my feet. Had to see you. We had to meet."

"You speak in rhymes," Kyle noticed.

"Rhymes and mimes always sublime. Words are here, words are there, but chemistry proves you're anywhere. Make the potion that reveals all, find the ingredients, stay out of the hall!"

"Stay out of the hall?" asked Kyle, somewhat confused. He pulled out the list, "I can barely read all that stuff on the list. How am I supposed to make a potion?"

"The potion that reveals all," Enov repeated. "Make the potion, do not waste, a disparaging notion, but you must haste."

"This potion," started Kyle, "is it in a bottle or..."

"You must make it. Find the ingredients, then you must take it to the last challenge on your list, but beware, the creatures in the mist." With that, Enov pointed to a door that was near the window. "Go through there to find the key, the ingredients and the vial that you'll need," and again, Enov disappeared.

Kyle looked at the door then back at the laboratory. The lab he was in seemed old, and even with all the tools and bottles, it appeared that he would find nothing in there. He opened the door and saw what he thought was a more modern laboratory.

Tables with early versions of the Bunsen burners, cabinets full of bottle and boxes presumably of chemicals, scales, weights, microscopes, as well as beakers, test tubes, flasks, other burners, and faucets. Two tanks marked OXYGEN and NITROGEN, were placed near the door. Two more tanks marked HYDROGEN and ARGON, were placed at the far side of the lab. More drawers were spaced at the ends of each table. He looked at the first one.

Papers from years ago were placed haphazardly in each drawer. Scribbles were on more of them as well as mathematical equations, evidently to figure out some other formula. No books, not even a desk reference of chemicals was on the desk

He looked at the tables. Each test tube looked clean. The flasks looked new and shiny. A table centrifuge was in the center of one table and was without rust or stains. Everything looked brand new.

Kyle turned to the cabinets to see if anything on the list was there. He pulled out the list and looked for the glycerin 134-n. The first cabinet was full of potassium, calcium, sodium, and bicarbonates. The second cabinet had three bottles of glycerin but no number 134-n. He continued to look and in the back row on the top shelf was a bottle marked Glycerin 134-n.

He pulled the bottle down and smiled. "One down," he said. He looked around the lab for anything else. Vials were plentiful so he grabbed one.

He looked for the Piterenneli 837 and Fermicycline Dioxide 35. The next cabinet seemed to hold nothing more than dyes and various liquids in unmarked bottles. The next shelf in the cabinet had bottle marked in chemical equations, like $CuSO_4$, $Cu(NO_3)_2$, and a bottle with a gray powder with a cracked piece of paper that was simply marked with a W.

Something about that struck Kyle. He had remembered something about tungsten and the letter W. He looked at the bottle and then it hit him. From back in third grade when his grandfather taught him about metals while he stayed with him on his farm. Tungsten has the symbol of W, which stands for Wolfram. "So, this is a bottle of tungsten," he said. "Two down." And with that, he placed the bottle of tungsten next to the bottle of glycerin 134-n and the vial.

But he needed something to carry everything if he was to proceed to the next challenge. He looked in the closet and found an old-style doctor's bag and placed the items inside. "Okay, now we're getting somewhere," he said as he looked at the list.

The list included petals of different plants and flowers. He figured that those would be obtained in the maze garden and perhaps by the pond. But the other stuff had to be in the lab, he thought. He continued his search for Ferrous Oxide, Tri-lydaremocous and Fermicycline Dioxide 35. Remembering his grandfather, he knew that Ferrous Oxide was rust. He could find rust practically anywhere but also felt that any lab would have a bottle, or at least a rusty can. That's the next ingredient, he determined. At least he knew what that was.

As he looked for a bottle of rust, he found the mirror. The mirror had a groove etched into the center of it that went down the middle of it. As he read the directions, he thought that the groove was to direct the flow of something to the bottom of the mirror. What did the directions say? *"Capture the light of the Lampyridae with the mirror coated in Essence of Newberry. Their bioluminescence will be captured in the Newberry."* Now to find out what a 'Lampyridae' was.

He found a dictionary on another desk and looked up the peculiar word. "Hmm, a Lampyridae is Latin for a firefly," he said, paraphrasing the definition. "So, I have to catch the bioluminescence of a firefly." He looked around. "Hey, Enov. It says I have to catch that lightning stuff in fireflies with a mirror. How many fireflies, and do I have to kill them?" He didn't expect Enov to return to answer him as that would probably be seen as cheating. Instead, he continued to go through the bottles for all the other ingredients.

More items that weren't on the list were found. The lab seemed fully stocked for a chemist, but nothing else would be of use to him. Finally, he found a bottle of Ferrous Oxide, the rust he needed for this weird potion. Now for the rest.

He now had Ferrous Oxide, an etched mirror, Tungsten, and Glycerin 134-n, and a bag to hold everything. Still a long way to go. Even missing one ingredient would cause him to fail. Apparently, the rest of the items would be found elsewhere.

CHAPTER FOUR
THE THIRD KEY

Kyle reached the bottom of the stairs and was met by a double door. The hallway wasn't like upstairs, where it ran the full length of the house. Instead, the hallway ran from front to back of the mansion. He tried the door expecting it to be locked. To his surprise, the door opened with a simple push.

The room was big, bigger than the library and bigger than both laboratories put together. Items such as chairs and other furniture were placed in one area. Dressers, trunks, mannequins of clothing, all gave the room the appearance of the back room of a department store. Most of the windows were covered by old drapes and curtains, while others were blocked by tall dressers, curios, and china cabinets.

What was he to find in here? He thought that some of the remaining ingredients must be old medicines that had long since disappeared from the pharmacy store shelves. He decided to look for Ambrosialydermacline since, to him, it sounded like something a woman would put on her neck. He checked the dressers for a small jar of Ambrosialydermacline but found, instead, jars of ointments for pain and perfumes with names that used French words.

He also decided to see if there was a bottle or jar of Fermicycline Dioxide, since that also sounded like a medicine. More dressers were lined up against the wall by the windows and he decided to check each one. Most of the dressers had old clothing of silks and cotton. The upper drawers had combs, hairbrushes, hair creams, colognes, and more perfumes. He continued looking and searching until he found a small bottle with the name Henney's Fermicycline Dioxide 35. Another item down, he said to himself.

As he looked in the next dresser, a twinkle to his right caught his eye. He looked over and saw two bright white lights shining off a dress. He walked to the light and saw that a red patterned dress hanging on a mannequin had something coming out of a pocket. It was a gold chain with two small diamonds on it that was reflecting the sunlight. He pulled on the chain and out came a locket in the shape of a heart.

He opened the locket and found the face of a beautiful young girl on one side but nothing on the other. For a slight moment, he felt a bit of sadness for the girl. He smiled at her beauty before closing the locket. But it seemed like he had seen the face before. It was in the family journal.

He pulled out the journal and looked for the girl's face. He found it, Amelia Douglas. She was born in 1814, was cousin to Simon Chadwick, and lived in the mansion until she, disappeared? He read on...

Amelia Douglas, born 1814 – died ??, was the only child of Myrtle and Tobias Douglas. She was an apt student, excelling in all subjects. She learned the art of being a lady from her mother, and also learned how to draw and paint. She had measles when she was 4, mumps when she was 7, but had no other serious diseases. Her parents died when she was 12 when their carriage was thrown over the side of the bridge just down the hill from the mansion.

"So that's why there's a plaque at the bridge," thought Kyle to himself.

The mansion still conducted Festivals which were run by Simon Chadwick, the cousin of Amelia Douglas. On the day of the Festival of 1828, Amelia was given the keys to the cellar. That was the last time Amelia was seen.

Some say Amelia ran away from Sevenoakes Manor. Others say she was killed, and her body hidden. As of this writing (1861), no one has seen Amelia Douglas nor knows what's happened to her.

As he was about to return the locket to the dress, a voice from behind took him by surprise. "Excuse me," said the voice.

"Enov?"

"No, no, not Enov. I'm Gladys." With that, the person emerged from behind a bed. She was older, short, and dressed almost in the same style of clothing as Enov.

"Gladys?" said, Kyle. "You know Enov?"

"Yes, I should," she said. "He is my husband. I'm sure that he told you that I'm supposed to help you keep your stride."

"Uh, yeah, he said something like that."

"Well, it's true. So, here's my advice. Keep that locket with you. The girl you're looking at is the Matriarch. She's the one you need to rescue."

"She's very pretty," he said, studying her picture. "But I thought I was supposed to rescue everybody," he said.

"You are, and if you do it right, you'll be able to rescue everyone in the mansion, her included." Kyle looked at her, questioningly. "The Judge told you that you needed all ten keys in order to get everyone out of here. But he didn't tell you about the Matriarch. She's the object of The Festival, and I'm sure Je Rouge conveniently left out that little tidbit of information. So, get on with it, kiddo!"

"I am, I am, but what am I supposed to look for in this room?" he asked.

"What do you see?" she asked with a hint of a smile.

"Beds, dressers, I've been going through the dressers looking for items on this list," he said, showing Gladys the list of ingredients. "And I found this locket that you told me to keep."

"Well, there you have it! You found some things for that potion and you've found the locket. Your challenge is done, and you can proceed to the next one," she said. "But you must remember not to take the next one too seriously. Do not let the next challenge get into your head. What you will see can't be described if you let them get into you. Only looking at them from afar can you describe what you see.

Otherwise, you'll be cursed to see all sorts of foulness and evilness. Just do not let them get to you," she warned.

"What are they? How do I fight them?"

"I told you, don't let them get into your head. Take them for nothing more than..." she stopped herself, "but I've said too much already." She looked up at him. "All right, be off with you and win this challenge!" And with that Gladys turned to stone then disappeared.

Kyle put the necklace on and tucked the locket under his shirt. At least it would be safer around his neck than in his pocket, he thought. He took the items he had found in the dressers and walked toward the door.

Suddenly, a rumble was felt to his left. He turned to see a dresser wobbling forward and backward. The top drawer slid slightly open, and a burst of yellowish light was scene. When the dresser stopped moving, the glow faded. Kyle looked inside and found the second key.

CHAPTER FIVE
THE THIRD FLOOR

The door slammed shut behind him as he stepped out into the hallway. He had seen the hallway before but this time, something just didn't appear right. The wallpaper, at first, appearing like red ivy and flowers, now looked like faces and ghostly patterns.

Kyle stopped and looked at the walls. They seemed to be moving, as if coming to life. All was silent around him. Even the birds outside the window became silent. The hallway grew dark as the light from the windows faded, though it was just after 3 o'clock.

From his right came the sound of heavy breathing. "Hello?" he asked but received no answer. The breathing increased to the point that a moan was heard.

Whispers from his left startled him. "Who's there?" he asked, almost in a demand. He tried to make out what they were saying but they sounded too much like noises instead of anything intelligible.

"Kyle," came a whisper.

"What," he said, feeling fear starting to grow up his back.

"Kyle," another voice sang out, followed by several more voices all saying his name.

"What!" he demanded this time.

The voices all said his name, but one was clear, "You are the one, the one picked by Je Rouge."

"Yes, I, uh, guess I am," said Kyle.

"Death will be brought to you if you proceed further!"

"What do you mean?" asked Kyle, trying to steady his nerves.

A high-pitched voice spoke, "Leave here and never return! If you go to the pond, all will be lost."

"You must leave Sevenoakes Manor immediately. Your life depends on it!" another voice warned.

"I can't leave! I'm here now. I was adopted!"

"You were chosen, picked among others to participate," a deeper voice said.

"Go and leave us!" said more voices.

Suddenly, the shapes on the walls turned into faces, each displaying pain and horror. "You must give up! You must leave!" they said.

"What if I don't? How will I die?" he asked, trying to remember Gilda's warning about not letting them get into his head.

"You'll die a thousand times over if you stay here!" warned another voice.

"You must leave!" said the face of an old man. "Leave at once!"

"I can't leave!" protested Kyle.

"You will die!" said a woman. Just then a vase fell off a table and crashed to the floor.

Images of Sevenoakes Manor flashed across the wall. Children in the yard, there one moment, lying on the grass the next, caused Kyle to look away. Lightning streaked across the mansion while thunder was heard outside. The voices of the long dead were still yelling for Kyle to give up and screaming Kyle's name.

"There's no shame in quitting, Kyle! You must save yourself!" said another man.

"I have to stay," said Kyle. "I'm going to see this to the end."

"Stay and you'll die!" warned another old man.

"Kyle," sang the voice of a woman. "The end for you is near!"

More images appeared on the wall. Images of bats appeared to fly at him. Rapid dogs, all foaming at the mouth, barked and lunged at him. An image of a young boy from all those years ago, waved a sword at a horse. In the next instant, the horse was running wild and pulling a carriage of screaming people.

Lord Elwin's face appeared stern like a businessman. Suddenly he was clutching his throat and gasping for air. A gravestone appeared with his name on it. Other gravestones appeared with the names of Louis, Tobias, Myrtle, and others Kyle had read about in the journal.

Images then appeared of children playing then screaming as they turned to stone. The daylight on the wall was bathed in red as the stones fell over. This caused Kyle yell in protest.

A fire erupted from the wall. The flames seemed to be too real to be just an image. Kyle could feel the heat as each flame seemed to lash out at his body.

"Run Kyle! Leave all behind and run!"

"No! I will not give up!"

From the center of the wall, the old and withered face of a man appeared. His eyes were gone leaving black holes in his head. "Go away! Save yourself! The end for you is near if you don't run. Now go!"

"Kyle, you can't stay here! You must go!" said another woman.

"You said I would die if I stayed," said Kyle. "How will I die?"

Just then, a vision on the wall showed a ghostly figure of a large monster coming out of the pond. The smell of decay was strong as water dripped from the monster's body. Kyle covered his mouth and nose in an attempt to stop the smell from invading his nostrils and making him sick.

"He will kill you! Go away now and avoid that which lurks in the pond!" warned the voices.

Light from the end of the hallway caught his attention. Suddenly, knives and spears were coming at him, their points slicing through the air. He dodged a knife, then a spear, then another and another. "What is this?" Kyle yelled. More knives and spears continued to fly toward him. One passed so closely that he felt the breeze as it went by. "Stop it!" he yelled to no avail. More screams and yells of warnings were heard but the knives kept coming at him.

Kyle picked up a small chair and threw it at the oncoming weapons but each one seemed to disappear only to reappear and head toward him. He fell to the floor to miss a spear, rolled to his side to miss a knife then jumped up to miss two more knives.

Faces appeared to be coming toward him, all laughing and mocking him. He instinctively picked up a spear that was stuck in the floor and hurled it at the face. The face disappeared but more faces followed. He used the spear as a sword and sliced through the images. Each one moaned then disappeared. More laughter and more faces came toward Kyle as he fought them off. Images of people he had never seen before appeared.

Then as fast as they appeared, the spears and knives stopped. Instead, images of Lord Elwin reappeared. He was standing by his lab table. The picture of his brother, Louis, appeared as it was in the family journal. The rest of the family members appeared, but now their faces seemed distorted. Some faces were bulging out while others seemed skinny on one side and wide on the other.

"Kyle," said a voice that appeared to be coming from Lord Elwin, "stop the challenge. Give up The Festival. It's not worth it."

"Why do I need to stop?" he asked.

"Kyle, stop the challenge or you shall die!" followed by a maniacal laughter.

"Kyle," another voice moaned, "you must stop, you must! All that you've done is meaningless. All that you'll do will be fruitless. Give up and stop the challenge."

"No!" yelled Kyle.

"You must!" laughed a woman. "You are no good to anyone when you're dead! You must stop this!" she said as she continued to laugh.

Another loud voice boomed with laughter over the rest. The images of the Chadwick family disappeared as the laughing face of Je Rouge appeared, causing Kyle to step back near the top step of the stairs.

"Stop!" yelled Kyle. "None of you are real! None of this is real!"

And with that, the hallways were silent. The lamps on the walls slowly grew brighter. Kyle looked around. No spears, no knives, the broken vase was intact. All the chairs and small tables were untouched, even the one he threw.

CHAPTER SIX
THE SECOND FLOOR

Kyle found himself on the second floor. All faces and all ghosts were gone. He looked around to make sure that he was alone. He heard a vibrating sound coming from a small table underneath a light. The table started moving until the top drawer opened. With a bright yellowish glow, Kyle knew he had another key. He pulled the key out of the drawer and added it to his growing collection.

The hallway was long as the ones upstairs and was lined with doors and lights. More small tables were sporadically placed down the hall. He decided not to look in the tables but rather see if any of the doors were open. He tried the first one and found it to be unlocked. He opened the door and entered what appeared to be a long bedroom that spanned the equal length of the hallway. Beds were in two neatly placed rows with nightstands on one side of them and closet dressers on the other.

He walked down the middle of the beds. As he walked, he looked for more signs of his next challenge. Nothing was obvious to him. He tried a closet, then another but found little in the way of direction. Instead, he found old undershirts folded and placed properly next to underwear. Other garments of clothing were either folded or hung in the closet. Drawers held socks, more underwear and shirts, and some toiletry items.

Kyle closed the door and walked to the next one. He heard a noise behind him. He turned around. "Enov? Gilda?" he asked, expecting to see them. He heard noises from the other direction and turned to see several statues of boys all about his size and age. "Who are all of you?"

he asked with a hint of fear in his voice. One by one, each statue cast a bluish-white glow and became real.

The boy closest to him had red hair, black pants with suspenders and a white shirt. "It's all right, you're among friends," he assured Kyle.

"Who are you?"

"I'm Preston Hunt," he said. "I was one of the challengers."

"So was I," said a black-haired boy. "David Coleman."

"Me, too, in fact, all of us were challengers," said another boy.

"What happened to all of you?" asked Kyle as he looked at them.

"We all lost at different challenges," said Preston. "I lost it in the hallway of faces."

"I lost it out at the pond," said David.

"Me, too," said another boy.

"I lost it in the Conservatory," said a pudgy boy with glasses.

"What happened?" asked Kyle.

The pudgy boy sat on the bed. "I was trying to find the song. All the instruments were floating over my head. When I found the song that any girl would like, I selected it." He looked down. "Mister Je Rouge came in and laughed at me and told me that I had failed."

"I was in the Dining Room when the flying creatures got me," said another boy. "When I woke up, Je Rouge told me that I had lost, and I was sent here."

"I lost my challenge in the Laboratories," said another.

"The basement," another boy spoke up.

"How long have you all been in here?" asked Kyle.

Preston looked at Kyle. "What year is this?"

"What year?" asked Kyle, taken back by the question.

"I lost my challenge in nineteen sixteen."

Kyle looked around as the other boys said the year when they had lost... 1907, 1921, 1914, 1942, 1935, 1956, 1963 were some of them.

"I made it this far," said Kyle. "What can you tell me about the other challenges?"

"We can't tell you how to pass them," said Preston, "only what we did wrong. Take our errors but do not repeat them."

Then it dawned on Kyle about Je Rouge. "So, wait, Je Rouge was around back then?"

"Mister Je Rouge has been around since before Melvin Horton won The Festival," said David.

"That was one-hundred fourteen years ago," said the pudgy boy.

"Wait a minute. Are you telling me that Mister Je Rouge, the man who adopted me yesterday, is over a hundred years old?" asked Kyle in disbelief.

"Older than that," said a tall boy. "I'm Raymond. I was brought here after Melvin had won. Even back then, in nineteen seven, Diabolos Je Rouge was running this place. He has a long history here at Sevenoakes."

"But he wasn't always known by that name," said a boy standing behind Raymond. "He changed it many years after the deaths of the family members that owned Sevenoakes."

"The one survivor took over. Once he inherited the estate," said Preston, "he tried to keep the family business running in his name so that he could continue to practice alchemy."

"That brought on suspicions from the local people," said another boy.

"So, he acquired another business partner and turned everything over to him," said the pudgy boy.

"Acquired another business partner?" asked Kyle. "Sounds like one of those weird shows on TV."

"I remember those," said a voice from behind. "I'm Jasper. I lost in nineteen seventy-seven, down by the pond." Jasper walked closer to Kyle. "Je Rouge is indeed as evil as they come. When the people started to take notice to a fifteen-year-old boy running a mansion and family business, and refusing the help of bankers and other people, they started to question his innocence in the deaths of Lord Elwin and the rest of them."

"The girls know a little more about Je Rouge," said David.

With that, the bedroom door opened and in came seven girls, including the two from dinner.

"I'm Rebecca," said the first girl from the table. "Kyle, if there was some way of getting out of the challenges, we would tell you."

"We can't interfere, but only tell you about the past Festivals," said the second girl from the table.

"And who are you?" asked Kyle.

"I'm Delilah," she said with a frown. "I've been here since it all started over two-hundred years ago."

"But I thought this Melvin guy released everyone but the Matriarch. Are you the Matriarch?"

"I am not."

"She's in another part of the mansion," said a third girl. "She was the first girl at Sevenoakes, back before Simon inherited the mansion. Mister Je Rouge has her encased in light."

"What?" asked Kyle. "This is getting weirder and weirder all the time!" he said to himself.

Delilah spoke up, "When the Festivals first started, there was a young boy who participated. He wasn't very good and kept losing most of the games we played. That boy was Simon Chadwick." She paused. "Then Lord Elwin passed away and The Festival stopped one year. Simon expelled all the orphans but kept only a few. I was one of the few he kept. We stayed to take care of the mansion and the grounds. Everything was nice, but after the year was over, Simon became obsessed with winning and started The Festival. The first girl living here disappeared during that Festival."

"Yeah, I read about it in the journal," said Kyle.

"He started it up again," said a fourth girl, "but only for those living here. The following year, I was brought in along with the rest of the girls."

"And we all played the games, sang the songs, and competed in every challenge," said Delilah. "Simon added more complicated challenges that only he could win. The boys who played against him all lost."

"That's when we started seeing statues that looked like the boys being placed around the mansion," said the fifth girl.

"How was that possible?" asked Kyle.

"Simon was heavily involved in alchemy and he started to show an interest in black magic," said Delilah. "And it's true that he acquired a business partner. That partner's name was Diabolos Je Rouge."

"What happened to Simon?" asked Kyle.

"Simon turned the business over to Je Rouge. When his interest in alchemy took over, he made incredible games with creatures that were then unimaginable," said Delilah. "And after years of running the business from home and Je Rouge running the business in the city, Simon decided to buy his competitors. Some say that the potions he made kept draining his bank account, so he needed more money. He grew the business all through the Caribbean and deeper into Europe."

"But his potion to keep Je Rouge in the eyes of the public started to work too well. Je Rouge slowed down his aging. He became one that ages in days while others aged in years," said Rebecca.

"So, Je Rouge was used by Simon, who also stopped him from aging," said Kyle, thoughtfully. "But what happened to Simon? There's no date showing when he died in the family journal."

"Correct," said Jasper.

"This may sound crazy, but is he still alive?"

"Simon is dead," said the pudgy boy.

"So, what happened? What was he doing? Is he the one who got Je Rouge to do these festivals? And if so, why?"

"Your questions are irrelevant. However, Diabolos Je Rouge has to win at everything, just like Simon," said Delilah.

"And by losing, you become a statue like us," said Preston.

Kyle thought for a moment, "Je Rouge uses black magic in these challenges?"

"He has," said the pudgy boy, "but now Je Rouge runs The Festival. He's also using black magic, but nothing new since Melvin's time."

"This is getting wild," exclaimed Kyle. "I'm about halfway done with the challenges and I find out that the man running the festival has been around since the son of Lord Elwin's sister was alive." He thought for a moment. "I bet Je Rouge killed Simon, Lord Elwin and the rest of the family just so he could get the mansion and everything."

"That has been the belief among all contestants since they found out Je Rouge's true intentions," said Jasper.

"So how do I win against him?"

"You win against him by beating him," said David.

"You win by winning," said the pudgy boy.

"No other way to beat him other than winning the challenges," said Rebecca.

"Kyle, you have to keep going, not only for us, but for yourself." Preston walked to Kyle and touched his arm. "If you fail, you'll live out eternity in this room with us."

"But if you win," said David, "you'll free us all and you'll be free as well."

"Take the key," said the pudgy boy, pointing to the other end of the bedroom. "Go forth and be successful."

Kyle looked at the boy and then to where he was pointing and walked past the other boys. A dresser started to shake and soon the top drawer was open revealing the key. Kyle picked up the key, smiled, then put it in his bag. When he turned to thank the boys and girls, all were gone. The room was as he had found it with beds and closet dressers.

CHAPTER SEVEN
THE FIRST FLOOR

Kyle left the bedroom, ran down the stairs, and stopped. He was on the first floor. The bag of keys he had in the bag with the ingredients was weighing on his hand, but he knew that another challenge would appear soon. He adjusted the bag so that it had a better balance and headed toward the dining room.

The doors were closed and locked, at least from the Ball Room entrance. He walked to the foyer and saw the gated doors closed but unlocked. He opened them and walked through. The dining table was dark as no candles were lighted. The table was bare, except for the tablecloth. Around the room, the serving tables were cleaned and standing in their places by the wall.

Kyle slowly walked to the Ball Room doors, scanning the floor and wall, looking for any hint of the next challenge. No statues to guide him. No pictures to mock him. Nothing at all to help, nor hinder him.

When he reached the doors, he looked toward the other end of the Dining Room. The big mirror on the wall reflected the entire table and Kyle appeared miniscule in the reflection. He walked to the other end of the table until he looked up and saw himself in the mirror. "What kind of festival is this?" he asked himself again. His face looked tired, the tie and jacket had long since been discarded leaving him with only the white shirt and black dress pants.

As soon as he looked away from the mirror, four objects, floating in the air, appeared at the far end of the table. Kyle was frightened by the hovering objects. Behind him was the door that led to the kitchen, but before he could turn to go through it, all four objects flew toward him.

The objects were black spheres with a white glow to them. They appeared to Kyle as being black softballs. One flew past him leaving a hot sensation on his right cheek. Kyle tried to run through the door, but the other objects blocked his way. He ran down the length of the table and ended up at the Ball Room doors. He fought the doors, but their locks refused to release, trapping him.

He looked around for anything he could use to fight off the flying objects but found little in the way of any weapons. Vases, platters on the serving tables, plates and cups were the only things at his disposal. He picked up a platter and threw it like a disc at one of the objects. The platter hit the object causing it to explode then disappear.

"Flying meatballs taken down by a platter." He tried to pick up the platter again, but the other objects flew at him. He crouched under the table as they passed him by. From his vantage point he could see the dishes. He was directly in the middle of the table with the objects to his right and the dishes to his left. He rolled out from under the table and made a leap toward the dishes.

Opening the cabinet door, he grabbed a dinner plate and threw it at the objects. He continued until he hit one of them, sending it into a dusty mist. The other plates missed, but now the kitchen door was free. He ran through, found a chair, and blocked the door.

The kitchen was old looking with both a gas and electric stoves. Two baker's ovens were to their left. Refrigerators were to his right and the sink was in the middle. On the stove was a big pot; apparently a remnant from the lunch that he had missed.

A series of loud thumps was heard from the kitchen door until the door opened. The two remaining objects floated in, seemed to hover for a brief moment, then darted toward Kyle. Out of fear and reflex, Kyle picked up the pot and tossed the contents at both objects, soaking them, and causing them to fall to the floor before disappearing in a poof of black dust.

"Meatballs and broth," he snickered. "A delectable combination!"

He left the kitchen and walked out to the Dining Room and into the foyer. He thought about what had transpired. What exactly was the challenge? Fighting off flying meatballs? Making a mess out of the dining room and kitchen? Where's the key? He walked on until he was in the Ball Room. Off from that room was the Conservatory. He wandered inside.

The harpsichord and other instruments were exactly as they were before when Je Rouge showed him the room. He looked around seeing nothing that was an obvious challenge. But something else was in the room that wasn't there before. A familiar statue.

"Enov?" he asked the stone figure.

A second later, the statue came to life.

"What you seek is a series of keys," he said.

"Yes, I need all ten keys to win this festival."

"The keys you have are not the keys you need. The keys you have are not for thee. Find the keys to find the start, for what you seek comes from your heart."

"Do you always speak in rhymes?" asked Kyle.

"Rhymes and mimes, always sublime," he said with a smile. "Hurry and find the keys. But beware. The wrong keys will send things aflutter. And with that, the room will shutter making the notes you seek remote, to speak." And with that, Enov returned to stone.

Kyle thought for a moment and repeated the hint, "Find the keys to find the start, for what you seek, comes from... the heart." He remembered the locket and pulled it out. He opened it again and found the old picture of Amelia on one side and nothing on the other. Amelia was "alone" in the locket. But what could this have to do with the Conservatory? he asked himself.

"Key, keys," he said to himself as he pulled out the bag of keys from the ingredients bag. "None of these keys," but it dawned on him. "No, not these keys, but musical keys!" He looked at the harpsichord. "But, which ones?"

He thought back to his piano lessons and picked a key. As he played the note, a violin rose up from the chair it was on and began to float in the air around the harpsichord. "Things aflutter," he repeated the Enov's warning. He tried the C key and another violin rose and started to follow the first violin. He tried D and the cello rose and took flight behind the violins. He was afraid to try the B minor note for fear that the bass would start to fly. Instead, he tried the key of G. A piccolo rose and followed the other instruments. He tried the E key which made his fear realized; the bass rose and circled the harpsichord. Two more incorrect notes sent even more instruments flying above him and the harpsichord.

"Okay, you can all come down now," he said to the flying musical instruments. He looked at the chairs and saw one flute still sitting comfortably. He banged on the keyboard hitting multiple notes and it, too, went flying.

He looked at the small bookcase behind him and found several pages of sheet music. All the older classics from Bach, and Beethoven, to Mozart and Strauss were arranged neatly as if in order to be played as an upcoming recital. As he looked at the music, he noticed that every sheet was hand-written. There were no copyrights, no printing from some music company, nothing that would indicate the music was printed elsewhere. Whole chords, notes, all the major and minor symbols, all written by hand in all the detail of the original manuscripts.

He looked at one song and read the chords as Bm, Gm7, A, E, C, D7, and other notes. Strong feelings written into each song, as well as subtle lullabies. But he was missing something. What was it? What did Enov say about keys being close to the heart?

Amelia's locket, musical keys... he was at a loss.

He looked at the sheet music on the harpsichord. All the notes and all the chords meant something to their respective songs. Each played a part in the make-up of that particular song. "But how does all this help me?"

He picked up one song that had chord names written on It. One was Am, followed by an F and then a Gm7. AmFGm7, meant nothing. But it did stand out to Kyle. "A, m, that's A minor," he said. "There is an E chord, Am, and E." He continued to look. Another A chord and he had Am, E, and A. That looked like Amelia, but what about the "li"? He read further down the sheet and found a chord with the notation "ii" next to it. The first "i" looked to be longer than the next one. Kyle could make it out as an "l" if he didn't know better. He placed the music next to each other and that rounded out Am-E-li-A, or Amelia.

He played the chords and one by one the instruments descended back to their resting places and the harpsichord and the other instruments started playing a waltz based on those chords.

When the song finished, the harpsichord opened, revealing the strings inside. The familiar glow of light emerged, and the next key appeared. Kyle took the key, and with a smile, he said, "Thank you, whoever wrote all the music!"

As he left the Conservatory, he was met with the familiar stone statue of Enov. "Go no further than that of the gate of the Maze, for Bob White will be waiting to help you complete the next phase. Take these words and search high and low, for the feathers are what you need to show. Bob White will be there leading the song. Hurry past the pool, don't take too long!"

"Who's this Bob White guy?" asked Kyle.

CHAPTER EIGHT
THE MAZE GARDEN

Kyle walked outside through the double glass doors in the Conservatory. The patio was brightly lit with the bulbs that were buried within the stone walls, as well as the flood lights from the mansion. He walked toward the pool, observing the water fountain that was in the center. The trees were also bathed in light as a decorative display, presumably for the adult guests Je Rouge had mentioned. He walked past and came to the edge of the pool area.

"Proceed no further," came a voice from behind. Kyle turned and saw a face in the pool. "No one shall go to the pond. Avoid it if you wish to live."

"What's so important about the pond?" asked Kyle. "Everyone is telling me to avoid it. Why?"

"Death will come to you, swift and assured. You must turn back and go back to the mansion. Proceed no further!" warned the face.

"What about the garden?" asked Kyle. "I still need to find some guy named Bob White."

"He is not there. If you must continue, stop at the edge of the garden, and proceed no further. Death awaits you."

"So, the garden is safe, but the pond is not." Kyle looked at the garden entrance. "What about the tunnel? I have to get something called a Newberry from there."

"The tunnel is also filled with death. You must avoid the tunnel and the pond. Hurry, turn back now and do not return!"

"Are you from the hallway? Because they all told me the same thing."

"Turn and go back! Go back!"

Kyle bent down and picked up a rock. "I don't think so," he said then tossed the rock into the pool, obliterating the face.

The entrance to the garden looked inviting enough with two statues each pointing the way inside. Kyle looked at the statues and waited for them to come to life. They remained silent. He poked them but their stone features remained still. Convinced that the statues were nothing more than statues he walked inside.

The message from Enov said that he had to meet someone names Bob White. He returned to the entrance and spoke out, "Bob White." Still nothing from the stone gate keepers. He returned inside and looked around for more statues that would come to life.

He walked through an arch that led to another part of the garden, and another arch. Five arches and five parts of the garden but nothing to indicate anyone, any statues, by the name of Bob White. Still, he trudged on. One arch led to a bigger area that had a bench. This was one of the waiting spots Je Rough had spoken about for when people waited for someone to find their way through the garden. A sign on a small pedestal was next to the bench. It read: *Know ye who sits upon this bench that this is the first of many such benches. Sit upon and reflect on the way ahead and prepare for the path you choose. For the way is full of splendor and life as the many songbirds will sing.* Kyle read the sign again in search of a clue, but nothing was evident to him.

He continued to walk until he reached a wall with paths leading left and right. Looking down each path, he chose the left path and followed it. Above, birds sang which Kyle thought was odd to hear birds singing at night. Squirrels and muskrats scurried across his path. He walked until the path led him to the right. More animals and bird song as he continued his walk.

Ahead was an opening and another bench. A plaque next to the bench revealed another message: *Stay upon the way ahead. Make certain you have the way back. Keep alert, listen to the forebodings, and stay aloof for the way ahead can bring untold results of pain or pleasure. Listen to the birds and feel their song.*

Kyle read the sign but found it to be more like the last one with little more than a warning and a direction to listen to birds. Another challenge that seemed to have little to do with The Festival. He continued to walk on as the birds sang.

He stopped and heard the birds. Some of the songs sounded like random chirps while others sounded like a calling. At some point, all the birds sang at the same time, creating more of an annoyance to Kyle than that of a soft song. A moment later, one bird would start singing. That song seemed to start the others. It sounded different to him and not the trill nor chirping of the others. Then the birds resumed their unorganized singing, and Kyle waited for them to settle down, for the conductor to sing out his solo before directing the others to start their parts.

Kyle continued to listen and soon was able to pick out the various bird songs. One song sounded like a typical bird with its 'cheep, cheep' sound. Another sounded like a series of chirps, like a loud cricket. Still another bird had a trilling sound.

When the birds quieted down, presumably to take a break between songs, one bird was heard. The distinctive sound of "Bob White" was heard. Kyle listened intently. "Bob White" came the bird's song with a variation of "Bob-Bob White."

"That's the bird!" he said with a smile. "Now, how to get it's feather." Kyle continued to listen to the bird until he was able to determine its location. He slowly walked toward the bird song until he saw the small tree the bird's nest was in.

Slowly he crept with his eyes looking at the nest and his ears focusing on the bird song. He climbed the small tree. When he got within arm's length of the nest, he thought that the bird might attack him. He shook the branch the nest was on and the bird flew out, leaving behind a feather. Kyle quickly grabbed the feather and climbed down, putting the feather in his bag of ingredients.

He left the tree and the "Bob White" bird and continued down the path. A clearing was up ahead, and Kyle decided to rest there and take inventory of all the items he had. But when he got to the clearing, a small building was standing in the middle surrounded by a circle of hedges.

Ivy was growing on the building. He picked some vines and placed them in his bag. He also found the lilac and daisies and picked those. Almost done with the list, he thought. Rhubarb and ragweed were the next items. Looking around, he didn't see anything like those growing anywhere. "Must be at the pond," he said to himself.

Kyle looked at the building and saw the dark brown door with a light overhead. He walked into the round building and saw several rows of plants in the center of the floor and a telescope pointing toward the stars. "Wait, when did this greenhouse get here?" he asked himself. Je Rouge never showed him this during their tour yesterday. Then again, they never walked through the Maze Garden. He looked around the room and saw benches lined up against the rounded wall. Each bench had several potted plants, flowerpots, and small bags of fertilizer. A filing cabinet was off to one side and a toolbox was placed neatly on one of the benches.

He looked through the telescope to see the various stars in the galaxy. "What am I supposed to do in here?" he asked himself. He placed his bag on a bench and continued to look around for any clue as to what the next challenge was to be. On the wall near the telescope hung pictures of the moon in various stages, Saturn, Jupiter, Mars, Venus, a small spot that was Mercury, and the sun in eclipse. Nothing captured his eye in terms of any challenge clues. On the wall behind him were pictures of trees, flowers, ivy, vines, and fields of sunflowers.

With a sigh, he turned to the bag and pulled out the family journal. He looked over the list of names and dates of births and deaths and saw again that Simon was missing his date of death. If he was still alive, he would be over two hundred years old. "No way!" Kyle said to himself. The boys and girls in that bedroom had to be wrong. Then again, they were all ghosts, and he saw a bunch of other ghosts before talking to them, and he just got out of the Conservatory with flying instruments, and the dining room with the flying meatballs... Maybe, just maybe, they were all correct and Simon is still alive. But... where is he? Is he really Je Rouge?

He continued to look through the book but found more entries about the construction of the garden and other things that showed home improvements. The pond was once smaller. It was increased in size in 1872. The tunnel was built between 1874 and 1875 "to provide shelter should one get caught out in the elements between the pond and mansion," said the book. The garage was built in 1906 to replace the one for carriages, and to accommodate the Rolls-Royce.

Later in the book was a description of the new family business. Simon was mentioned as having inherited everything from Lord Elwin and the rest of the family, and that he turned that fortune back into the family exporting business. This was done by buying out his employer when he was eighteen. The book went on to say that Simon kept most employees but fired the executive staff, opting to bring in his own people. A newspaper clipping read that this led to an investigation as to the money used to purchase the company. When it was found that Simon did use his family's fortune to purchase the company, it was proved that those accusing Simon of underhanded dealings were the ones spreading false accusations. As a result, they were all sued for "attempted character assassination."

Simon later expanded the company to include markets all over the Caribbean as well as more areas in France, England, Spain, Portugal, Italy, and Germany. The company was doing quite well for itself in those days. The company's stock was soaring and taking on new rivels. Eventually, Simon bought out two of his fiercest competitors.

Back at the mansion came stories of festivals. Boys from all over were, at first, invited to join and play for prizes. Later, under Simon's business partner, Diabolos Je Rouge, boys were adopted to be given a new start on life.

This small part in the family journal left out a lot, thought Kyle. Why would Je Rouge adopt boys to give them a new life only to have them compete in this insane festival? Kyle shook his head still trying to accept the fact that Je Rouge was someone that was over two-hundred years old. But what of Simon?

Could Simon still be alive? If so, where is he? Perhaps Je Rouge got too greedy and condemned Simon to eternity as a statue like the rest of the boys. Kyle's mind wandered in a flurry of questions and possibilities. He kept looking over the book, but nothing was written about Simon, except one entry dated March 5, 1845 that said Simon went out to sea. He was heading toward Bermuda when his boat, the *S.S. Polydorus*, sank.

So, Simon was dead after all. Dead out at sea when his boat sank off the coast of Virginia. But no one updated his date of death.

Kyle looked up at the pictures of the planets and thought about all that he had seen and done since he arrived at Sevenoakes. Everything was like being in a haunted house and he had to escape. The only way to do that was to win The Festival. Then what? He had his freedom and the freedom of all those players of the past who were now encased in stone and light. All this because Simon didn't like to lose. And now Je Rouge is running The Festival? It seemed all too surreal to Kyle. Yet, here he was, participating.

What's the next challenge? Something in the greenhouse had to be figured out, a puzzle had to be completed, but what? Kyle looked through the telescope again to see Jupiter still in the night sky though now on the edge of his viewing window. The Big Dipper was also present. He tried to move the telescope to find other celestial wonders but couldn't figure out how to make it work.

"What are you doing?" came a familiar voice from behind.

"Gladys?" he asked the stone figure.

The stone figure turned to human, and Gladys smiled. "You are doing a marvelous job on all your challenges," she said. "But remember not to wait too long. You still have the tunnel and the pond to win. Those challenges will be difficult at best."

"Yeah, about that," started Kyle, "it seems like everyone wants me to stay out of the pond area. Those ghost in the hallway and then the other boys in the bedroom. All of them warned me about it."

"The boys are concerned, yet they want you to win." She walked over to him. "The road ahead will not be easy," she warned. "You must continue and get the rest of the ingredients. They are located outside in the garden, in the tunnel, and the rest will be at the pond. But you must beware not to cause too much commotion in the tunnel or the pond. Be quiet and do not disturb anything you see. The tunnel is going to be a hard challenge, but what you'll find in the pond can be deadly."

"What will happen?" asked Kyle.

"You will be attacked and then Je Rouge will appear and tell you that you've lost. And then you'll be turned to stone."

"The ghosts were telling me to give up-"

"You can't give up. You must continue and win!"

"That's my goal in this festival, to win."

"Then you must continue," said Gladys. "I told you not to let them get into your head."

"They didn't," said Kyle, "I'm going to finish this thing and Je Rouge will just stand there watching me win."

"That's a good attitude," said Gladys as a glow of light enveloped her. "Continue with the challenges. Hurry, but be quiet!" And with that, she turned back into stone and was gone.

CHAPTER NINE

THE TUNNEL OF ACHEROS AND THE SEPULCHRAL POND

Kyle turned around and looked at the maze garden exit. All seemed quiet as no birds were heard. He looked ahead and started on the downhill path to the tunnel. Remembering Gladys' words, he was careful not to make any noises as he approached.

Soon, he reached a small gate that was half his size and stopped. The other side was dark. He quietly opened the gate and stepped through.

The tunnel had a sign to the right of the entrance:

TUNNEL OF ACHEROS

"Who or what is an Acheros?" he wondered. He stopped at the entrance and looked inside. Nothing, nothing but blackness. "A flashlight would be helpful right now," he said to himself.

Kyle slowly walked inside the tunnel until all light from behind him was gone. He stood still, blinking, trying to see anything ahead of him. Then an eerie glow was seen that seemed to bathe him in a greenish-bluish light.

He walked slowly to the source of the light. But instead of finding one source, he found several glowing objects that resembled glow worms and black lights. For a moment, he thought of the dance he and Timothy and the other boys at the orphanage attended. The way the black light appeared to make all white articles of clothing appear ghostly was like what he was seeing now with his white shirt.

The ingredient that he needed was in this tunnel, he thought. But where is it and how else could he see it without more light? He closed his eyes for what seemed to be five minutes then opened them again. He could see more now that his eyes were adjusted to the poorly lit conditions. Now he was ready to walk further into the tunnel.

He did notice several things on the floor by the tunnel walls. One looked like a table while the other objects seemed to be lumps of rock. He looked over the table and found two drawers. Opening one of them he found some tools and a flashlight. "Ask, and you shall receive," he said to himself. He turned it on and squinted at its brightness.

Waving the light around, Kyle looked at the other objects. They appeared to be statues, but unlike the statues of the boys and girls in the mansion. These looked small, grotesque, and barely finished. What were they?

Kyle shined the light on one and saw an evil-looking face. It reminded him of the gargoyles from the mansion. He looked at another, and a third and realized that these, too, were gargoyles. But what were they doing here? Was this the place they made them? If so, why would they be made here just to be carried uphill, through the maze garden, then to the mansion? Or maybe this was a place to store the older ones, probably rejected ones, he thought.

The tunnel was long and winding, with bigger spaces where the path curved. In these spaces were more rocks, metal plates and metal rods. Nothing hung from the walls. No lights from the ceiling, either. Kyle did notice that some areas of the wall was blackened, like a torch that had long since been placed there. Upon closer inspection, he could make out the holes used to hold up those torches.

Now to find what he needed on the list. Essence of Newberry, and he still had no idea what that was. He continued to look around the gargoyles for anything that might resemble it. Another table was in the corner of the bigger room. He opened the drawers and found old tools in one and drawings and plans on how to construct a gargoyle in the other.

Stone was cut with a hammer and chisel. The metal was melted and molded into the shapes of breast plates, shin guards, feet guards and helmets. The metal rods were used for the spears. But there was a smaller passage about how to animate the gargoyles should evil appear. Kyle could barely make out the wording but did see something about dipping the spears in a vat of Essence of Newberry.

Kyle looked around but saw no vats, not even a pot or barrel. He did see the gargoyles, some with and some without spears. Perhaps the spears were dipped in the solution to see if they worked, he thought. That couldn't be the case as it would be too easy. Still, he scraped the point of a spear with his thumbnail and found that black flakes were coming off. He searched the tools drawer for something that would work better as a scraper.

Finding an old chisel, he scraped the point of the spear and collected the flakes in the bag with the keys. He went to another spear then another until he had more than enough of the Essence of

Newberry. Satisfied that he had all but the last two ingredients, he turned to put the chisel back in the drawer. As he walked back to the table, he tripped over a rock and caught himself against the wall, but also dropped the chisel, sending a loud clang echoing throughout the tunnel.

He froze - knowing that he had to be quiet - and waited for the sound to stop reverberating and something to happen. He turned off the flashlight and stood still.

When the tunnel returned to silence, Kyle looked around and saw the gargoyles still in their places on the floor. He picked up the chisel and quietly returned it back to the tool drawer. As he did, he heard a moaning from the entrance of the tunnel.

The moan was followed by other moans, and all getting closer to him. Kyle turned to run out the other way when more moans were heard. He stopped and turned on the flashlight. Two gargoyles were waddling up to him, their spears drawn. He turned around and saw more gargoyles coming toward him.

Armed with only the flashlight, Kyle tried to run out by passing the gargoyles. He was taller than they were, but they had spears. He picked up rocks and threw them at the advancing gargoyles. But the metal on them deflected each rock. One of them hurled his spear at Kyle. Kyle dodged it and watched as it hit the wall, chipping off the rock.

"Oh, not good," he said aloud. He ran up to the nearest gargoyle and shoved it aside. Several more were behind the first gargoyle and all had their spears drawn, pointing them at Kyle.

He turned around to try to go out the way he came in. Shoving the gargoyles aside and dodging the spears, he reached the tunnel entrance. But before he could leave the tunnel, a gate dropped in front of him, blocking his escape.

He pushed on the gate but found it too firm in place to budge. He turned back around to see more gargoyles coming for him. Again, he shoved and pushed his way aside. He managed to take a spear from one of the gargoyles and used it to fight his way back through the tunnel.

When Kyle reached the first open area, more gargoyles waited for him. They tossed their spears at him, but he deflected them with the spear he had. One of the gargoyles got close to Kyle. With all his strength, Kyle picked up the gargoyle and threw him into the crowd of waiting attackers, making a way for himself through the tunnel.

Finally, Kyle could see the other end of the tunnel, but this, too, was blocked by more gargoyles and a gate. He stopped trying to see if there was a way he could get through.

Behind him the gargoyles waddled up to him, armed and potentially just as deadly. Now Kyle was trapped, and the gargoyles stopped their moaning and growls. They spoke to him, but he couldn't understand them. One of them poked him with the spear. When Kyle failed to do what it demanded, it poked him again.

What sounded like laughter to Kyle caused him to become afraid. "Look, I didn't mean to disturb you," he said but they didn't listen. "Let me go and I'll never bother you again," he pleaded, but they continued to poke at him with their spears. All of a sudden, they started walking toward the other end of the tunnel, pushing Kyle along the way.

They walked until they came to another open space. This one had a table with cuffs for ankles and wrists. The gargoyles led Kyle to the table and forced him to get on and lie down. "What is this?" he demanded. As more spear tips hit him, he got the message that his doom was apparent. "I'm going to die, in a tunnel, by stone trolls," he muttered to himself. The gargoyles fastened the cuffs to his wrists and ankles. Fighting them off, at this point, seemed fruitless.

A gargoyle who appeared to be the leader, stood on a stool, and looked at Kyle. He mumbled a few words and the others laughed. He placed his hand on Kyle's forehead and mumbled again, causing more laughter.

Then the leader pulled out a dagger and with both hands, held it over Kyle's chest.

"No! What are you doing? You can't kill me!" protested Kyle.

From up the tunnel, a loud scream was heard, like that of a screech owl. The gargoyles stopped laughing and looked in the direction from which they had come. Kyle looked up and from the way they were acting, they were all scared.

Suddenly, bigger gargoyles flew in, screeching, and waving swords at the smaller gargoyles. A fight broke out and the shorter gargoyles stabbed the bigger ones with their spears. The bigger ones continued to wave their swords, knocking the smaller ones to the tunnel floor.

Then one big gargoyle flew to Kyle and started unlocking the cuffs. "The Matriarch sent us to rescue you. Get out that way," he said, pointing to the opposite way they came in, "and get to the pond. Go!"

Kyle jumped off the table and made his way through the fighting gargoyles and out of the tunnel.

When he reached the end of the tunnel, he heard no noise of any fighting. He saw no lights from the tunnel, and it was like what he had experienced never happened. He turned and saw the pond.

The sign read:

SEPUCHRAL POND

Like the Tunnel of Acheros, this was new to him. The pond was more of a square than a typical rounded shape. Trees took up most of the back side of the pond. Cattails and other plants covered most of the shoreline. The water looked black, even for a moonless night. The ground he stood upon seemed sandy with areas of slimy mud.

Kyle did see the ragweed plant that he needs for the potion. He picked the flowers and looked around for his bag. Then it dawned on him: He left the bag in the tunnel.

The tunnel was his only way to the pond, and no doubt his only way back to the maze garden and to the mansion. Whatever awaited him back in the tunnel, he'd have to meet it and get the bag whenever he was done at the pond.

He looked around and found the rhubarb. He picked what he needed of the plant and placed it on the ground next to the ragweed. He turned back toward the tunnel and listened closely. Still, no sounds were heard. He decided to go back to get his bag. But when he got to the tunnel, something was keeping him from entering. He couldn't get through. Now he had to wait until he won the challenge at the pond before going back.

"Well, I got all the ingredients," he said to the pond. "What will you have me do as a challenge?"

He thought about calling out for Enov or Gladys. It seemed that they always show up before a challenge. He looked around but saw no statues or any humans other than himself.

"Looking for something to do?" Kyle turned to see Je Rouge sauntering up to him. "Lots to do here at night, young Kyle. You just have to look for it."

"I'm stuck on the next challenge. I don't know what to do," he said, hoping Je Rouge would have an answer for him.

"Oh, come now, Kyle," he said. "You've been doing well so far, winning at everything. Frankly, I don't know how you managed to last this long. Others have given up by now." He smiled at Kyle. "Since you beat all the challenges up to this point, why do you take the rest of The Festival as a win and go back to the mansion?" Kyle yawned. "See, you're getting tired already. Why not go back and rest in your new bed?"

"I can't. I have to win."

"But you've already won, don't you see?" said Je Rouge. "You've beaten the flying meatballs, as you called them, in the dining room. You picked the correct waltz, and I'm sure the Matriarch will love that one. You've made it past the hallway of ghosts, and you escaped those little beasts in the tunnel. And you found all the ingredients of the potion." He looked at Kyle. "Go home. Get some rest. You've won."

"I want to, but..."

"But what?"

"I have to win," said Kyle. "Every challenge I've faced in my life either ended as a win or a loss. I was never told to just 'give up and go home.' I have to win this. I have to see this through to the end," he said, looking Je Rouge in his reddish eyes.

Je Rouge took a grip on his walking stick but maintained a smile that sent shivers through Kyle's spine. "Now, young Kyle. You have nothing to prove with me. I know you've won. You can go home. It's right through the tunnel, through the maze, and past the pool. You know the way."

"If I do leave now," said Kyle, "what challenge am I missing out on?"

The question took Je Rouge by surprise. "What challenge?" He looked around. "Well, the pond is a treacherous place at night. I'm sure walking around it in the dark would be a significant challenge for you." Kyle looked at him, not believing the lie. "But you don't have to do any of that. All you have to do is go home."

"And end up a statue like the rest?"

"What?"

"Yeah, the boys in that haunted bedroom told me their stories. One even lost the challenge right here," Kyle said.

"Young Kyle, I assure you that your fate will not end like that. Just give up and go home and all will be viewed upon as completed."

But Kyle remained where he stood. "I've got to see this through."

"I'm telling you, Kyle, you need to go home and rest."

"If I do give up, what about the Matriarch? Will she still be trapped somewhere in the mansion?" asked Kyle, almost in a demand rather than a question.

"That, I'm sure, can be answered up at the mansion. And if you wish to see her, I can arrange that for you on another day." Je Rouge looked at Kyle for any weakness but felt that even this verbal challenge was won by the young Kyle.

"I'm playing this out," insisted Kyle. "I'm not giving up." With that, he turned his back on Je Rouge and looked out over the pond.

Kyle didn't hear it, but Je Rouge pulled a sword out of his walking stick. Once out, he held it down by his side out of Kyle's view. "All right, young Kyle. I'll show you something in the pond." He pointed to the middle of the water. "Look out over there and see the center tree." He raised the sword and steadied it behind Kyle. "That tree is something that all contestants must go to during The Festival. For that tree has a fruit growing from it that can only be enjoyed at night." He stepped back away from Kyle and prepared himself to thrust the tip of the blade in Kyle's back. "And it is part of the challenge, to obtain the fruit."

Suddenly, the surface of the water next to Kyle was broken and two black tentacles appeared. Kyle moved out of the way as the tentacles grabbed Je Rouge by his legs, pulling him toward the water.

Je Rouge yelled and stabbed the tentacles several times with the sword. Just then, the head of the creature appeared. "No Caspian, no!" yelled Je Rouge as he continued to fight.

Kyle stood in amazement at the fight between Je Rouge and Caspian.

The black water monster struck Je Rouge then picked him up and shook him from side to side. "Caspian! Stop this! Caspian, no!" But the monster only shook harder before pulling Je Rouge into the middle of the pond.

As Je Rouge disappeared under the water, several balls of light appeared beneath the surface. An explosion caused the water to rise up, knocking Kyle to the ground. Kyle stood up as the black water grew still. "Je Rouge?" he asked into the night, fearing his host was dead.

Could this have been the challenge, to fight the Caspian monster? Or was the challenge to prevent Je Rouge from talking him out of continuing the challenges? He didn't know but grabbed the ragweed and rhubarb then ran back through the tunnel to retrieve his bag of keys.

CHAPTER TEN
THE BASEMENT AND THE TENTH KEY

Kyle walked back into the mansion and stopped. The Caspian monster was something no one warned him about. Enov and Gladys never told him about such a monster. He was warned not to go to the pond, but those were the ones working on Je Rouge's side and wanting him to fail. But even the boys in the bedroom never said a word about such a monster. Then again, most had never made it that far in their challenges. He won against the tunnel and the pond, and that was all that mattered. Now he must proceed to the next challenges and those were in the basements.

Kyle walked behind the staircase until he found the basement door. Knowing that Je Rouge was now dead, he felt that he could easily win whatever challenges awaited him. He opened the door and found the light switch. Turning it on, he saw the red carpet trimmed in gold that covered the stairs. The basement below was also well lit and he could see the carpeted floor.

He walked down the stairs with the bag in his left hand. When he reached the bottom of the stairs he looked around. The basement was big but smaller than the floors up above. Lights were well-placed from the ceiling and rooms lined the walls. He looked at the doors and sighed, thinking that he would have to try each door to see which room the challenge was in.

Then something struck Kyle about the basement that was different. Though the family journal never mentioned it, the rooms before him looked added, like they were newer than the mansion itself. He walked to the end of the basement until he came to an opening.

A row of benches lined the two corner walls. The walls were unpainted except for a series of numbers and dashes. He looked around the area and saw old boxes, old crates, and even older barrels. Under the benches were even more boxes and old drawers. He tried to open one drawer, but it was rusted shut. Another drawer was filled with old tools that were aged beyond their usefulness.

Next to the drawers was a safe. Kyle looked at it and thought that the next key might be in there. He tried the wheel, but it was locked. The dial worked, but he didn't have the combination. He looked at the wall again to see if any of the numbers were the combination.

He tried the some of the numbers as they appeared in order on the wall, dropping off the third number in each three-digit group: 3-19-892, 6-222-78, 5-1-11, 18-27-0, 342-940-2, 80-7-21, 999-410-30, but nothing worked. He tried the different combinations again but dropped the first number in the three-digit group, and even a few random combinations but to no avail.

He remembered back to the earlier challenges and thought of the hints he was given. Enov told him about the second laboratory and the ingredients. Gladys told him about the locket and Amelia. Enov told him about the keys of music, not the keys he was collecting. The musical keys led him to Amelia's name. The girls in the bedroom had spoken about the original girl when Simon was running the festivals. That girl was Amelia.

"Something about Amelia is the secret to the combination," said Kyle. "But what?"

He thought long and hard. Could it be the date that Amelia was captured and turned to stone? He looked through the book but found no mention of any potion turning people into stone, let alone anything like that happening to Amelia.

Was it her birthday? Again, he looked but found no mention of Amelia in the book, only the year she was born, 1814. None of the numbers on the wall worked. Guessing would take up to 365 tries as there are 365 days in a year. He tried, 1-1-0, then 1-2-0 and then 1-3-0 before realizing that this would take longer than the twenty-four hours that he had to complete the challenges.

His hand reached for the locket. Would the date be in there? He opened it and saw Amelia's smiling face staring back at him. The other side of the locket was empty, but he opened it anyway. A small white piece of paper, possibly used as backing for when a picture was placed in there, fell out. He looked at both sides and found nothing.

He opened the side with Amelia's picture and took it out. The backing paper behind her picture had something written on it. Kyle stood and walked closer to the light. The date read: 3-27-1814. That must be it, he thought. He tried 3-27-14, and the wheel was able to turn. The safe was open and sitting there was another key.

Kyle had won all but the last key, and soon it would be time to make the potion. He put the picture back inside the locket and returned the necklace to his neck. Then he put the key in his bag and started to leave when he heard a loud sound of metal clanging.

At the end by the basement door stood a suit of armor. A feeling of fear and dread rose up Kyle's back as the suit slowly walked toward him. Kyle looked around for any weapon he could use.

The suit of armor raised its sword and started to walk more quickly toward Kyle.

"Enov, Gladys, if you're around, what do I do?!?" he asked while continuing his search for a weapon. He went back to the safe and looked around.

In the clutter of the boxes and crates, he found a knife but tossed it aside. He found a baseball bat but also tossed that aside. The sounds of the suit's feet were getting closer. He looked behind the barrels and found a spear made of metal. Both ends were pointed and appeared longer than the broadsword of the suit of armor.

"Aim for the neck, it is the weakest! Hurry now, or it's the bleakest!" said a voice from behind.

"Enov, if that's you," Kyle started, "I've never fought a suit of armor before."

"The weakest point is below the head. Aim for the neck, how Melvin did. Take the spear, for it's the sleekest. After he strikes, his neck's the weakest."

Kyle didn't see Enov vanish but instead concentrated on getting himself ready with the spear. The suit walked closer as Kyle stood, looking for the weakened point in the armor suit's neck. The suit raised the sword and brought it down swiftly and hard against the floor. A chip of tile flew from the stricken floor sending a chill down Kyle's spine.

Kyle saw his chance. If the suit would strike the floor again, he could run up and shove the spear through its neck. Kyle waited and watched as the suit of armor walked closer.

The suit of armor raised the sword with both hands, preparing to strike. Kyle darted out of the way as the blade fell within inches of his leg. Kyle struck the suit with the spear, causing no damage, but knocking the suit off balance for a split second.

The suit raised the sword about halfway and brought it down at Kyle, slicing his shirt and cause a red welt on the boy's stomach. The suit picked up the sword again and swung it toward Kyle, missing him. Kyle aimed for the neck but hit the suit's shoulder, the tip bouncing off and striking the face shield of the suit.

Kyle ran behind the suit and tried to hit its neck, but the suit turned too fast and was now facing him. Kyle ran up to the suit and shoved him, causing the suit to take several steps backward. The suit regained itself and poised for another attack. As it raised its sword, Kyle thrusted the spear in its chest. The suit fell backward and landed on the floor.

Kyle ran up to the suit of armor and shoved the spear into its neck. The suit shook violently. From the mesh and the armor joints were beams of white light. The suit of armor shook again until it fell apart.

The chest area of the suit was still glowing when Kyle stood over it. When the light faded, the final key was present. Kyle picked up the key and put it in his bag.

With the suit of armor now in a pile of metal, Kyle decided to pick up the sword and carry it with him to the sub-basement. Hopefully, this would be his last challenge. He had the keys, the ingredients, and had won all the challenges thus far. What he needed now was a place to mix the potion, and a weapon. He tried to pick up the sword but fell backward.

The sword wasn't that heavy, but fatigue had set in and now Kyle was tired and approaching exhaustion. He didn't have a watch and no clocks were nearby, but he felt that it was way past midnight. If only he could sleep... No, no, he had to keep going. He had to see this thing to the end.

Kyle picked up the sword and the bag and walked to the door that led to the stairs. The stairs leading to the sub-basement was dark except for a faint light glowing at the bottom of the staircase. He held onto the railing as he took each step cautiously.

Kyle reached the lower basement. He looked up to see the torches at the bottom of the stairs, and the other torches in the sub-basement as they started to come to life. He stumbled in and fell to the floor, feeling every ounce of strength leaving his body. He took a deep breath and pushed himself up off the floor, feeling the stinging on his stomach from the last challenge. Looking down he could see that his shirt was ripped and the long scratch on his stomach inflicted on him by the suit of armor, was bleeding. Seeing that the scratch was minor, he folded his shirt over and rubbed the drips of blood from his skin.

The familiar sound of a door closing came from behind. He turned to look to see Je Rouge at the door, carrying his familiar walking stick.

"Come in, young Kyle. Nice of you to... drop, in?" he said with a sardonic smile. Kyle looked up to see the Je Rouge practically laughing at him.

"What are you doing here?" he asked, noticing the blood on Je Rouge's hand. "I thought you drowned."

"Only swimming with an old friend, dear boy," he said as he wiped the blood from his hand. Then he slammed metal tip of the walking stick on the floor. "You have done well in this game, young Kyle. But you still have one more challenge, that you will fail. And then I can go on ruling the mansion and these grounds outside for another century!"

Kyle felt a strong wave of wind knock him down to the floor. "I have all ten keys. I will win!" he said as he picked himself back up.

"Oh, no, no, no, no, no," replied Je Rouge. "The other challenges were easy compared to this final challenge. The others were merely a test for you to collect the ten keys." He locked the door. "Now, you must choose the correct key, the one that will release the Matriarch, or the one that will keep her locked up."

A bluish glow appeared behind Kyle. He turned to see a stone statue coming to life. The statue was a girl. Could this be Amelia?

"Kyle, you must ignore Je Rouge and complete the potion. You must concentrate," said the statue that was now a girl, but was encased in light.

"Amelia?" asked Kyle.

"Yes, I'm Amelia. You must hurry and complete the potion. Everything you need is in this room," she said as she waved her hand.

Kyle looked at the bench beside Amelia. It looked to him like a much smaller version of the second laboratory he had seen earlier. Test tubes, mixing utensils and other tools were at his disposal. He put the bag on the bench and took out all the ingredients.

"That will do you no good, young Kyle," said Je Rouge. "What will you prove by making a potion?" Kyle paid no attention to Je Rouge. "You'll make a mess, nothing more." Again, Kyle was silent. "You can't possibly win by making that concoction. Give it up and concede defeat."

"No."

"Young Kyle, listen to me. This mansion has been here for over two centuries. You can't win against all that is here. Give it up and I'll personally take you back to the Cumberland Boys Home."

"Nope."

"You'll be with your friends again. You'll be with Timothy," offered Je Rouge.

"No." Kyle continued to mix the ingredients. To keep Je Rouge from talking, he turned to Amelia. "I have to know something," he started. "The others in the bedroom said that you were the first one in the mansion. What happened to Simon?"

"Keep quiet, Amelia," warned Je Rouge.

"It says in the journal that he died out at sea on his boat, the, uh, something or other."

"That is correct," she said. "The journal said that Simon Chadwick died at sea. But that's not the truth."

Kyle looked at Je Rouge.

"She lies," he said. "Simon died when the *Polydorus* sank off the coast of Virginia!"

"Kyle, there is more than Je Rouge is telling you. Simon turned me into stone and has me encased in light."

"Shut up, Amelia! Simon is dead. Let's not speak badly of him."

"You shut up, Je Rouge!" yelled Kyle. "Please continue," he said to Amelia.

"Simon was responsible for The Festivals, and turning others into stone if they failed," she said.

"Like me, if I don't finish this potion," said Kyle. He poured the liquid ingredients in with the dry ingredients and, following the instructions, heated up the potion.

"Young Kyle, I think you're wasting your time and energy," said Je Rouge. "Don't listen to Amelia. She's encased down here for a reason."

"What reason?"

"Kyle, I know the secrets. That's why Simon did this to me," she said with a tear in her eye.

"What secrets?" asked Kyle as he took the potion from the heat.

"Say nothing, Amelia, or what Simon did to you will be nothing for what I'll do to you!" warned Je Rouge.

"Tell me, Amelia," he said as he took the vial of potion to the table in front of Amelia. As he placed the keys on the table, Amelia spoke.

"Kyle, Simon was evil. When we were younger, he and I were cousins. Later, when his uncle, Lord Elwin, started to experiment with alchemy, Simon thought his uncle was wasting his time and the family fortune." She took a breath. "Simon killed Lord Elwin by poisoning him."

"What?" asked Kyle. He thought for a moment, "Did he kill the rest of his family?"

"Yes, all from poisoning them."

"That's a lie!" yelled Je Rouge. "A bold-faced lie!"

"No, it isn't. He poisoned the horse that killed my parents, Myrtle and Tobias. Every family member that died in eighteen twenty-six was killed from poison by Simon."

"Lies, lies. Everything she says is a lie!" yelled Je Rouge.

"It isn't." She took another deep breath. "I have one more secret. Diabolos Je Rouge is Simon Chadwick."

"Balderdash! She's obviously lying to you in order to confuse you!" Je Rouge yelled.

"She doesn't need to do that to confuse me, Je Rouge," said Kyle. "Besides, I have the potion and the keys ready."

"Then go ahead and use that flimsy potion and choose, if you think that'll help."

Kyle looked at Je Rouge then back at Amelia.

"Kyle, you must choose," she said, trying to hold back more tears.

Kyle poured the potion over the keys and waited. Nothing happened.

"See, I told you that the potion was worthless and that you are wasting your time," mocked Je Rouge.

Kyle picked up the third key, looked at it, then returned it back to the table. He picked up the fourth, fifth, and sixth keys, but none seemed to be the correct key. He looked at the Matriarch; his eyes screaming a silent plea for help.

"Choose, Kyle," said Amelia. "Time grows short!"

Kyle looked at the flat surface of the table, again, but saw nothing on or around the tabletop that would fit a key.

"Kyle," said Amelia with a caring smile.

Finally, Kyle picked up the fourth key, held it up to the Matriarch, and recited his declaration, "I, Kyle Edward Yates, do hereby... uh, hereby..." But he stopped. The seventh key started to vibrate and change color. That was the correct key. He smiled and held up the seventh key. With the key high over his head, he said, "The seventh key; The Festival takes place every seven years; the mansion is known as Sevenoakes... It has to be the seventh key," Holding up the seventh key, he looked at Amelia and felt a strong feeling of love for the encased Matriarch. Then he felt the answer come to him in a wave of enlightenment. He put the key back onto the table and announced, "I, Kyle Edward Yates, do hereby declare that I am the correct key!"

The table rumbled and each key suddenly turned red then bright yellow before flames grew and shot up toward the basement ceiling. The torches in the room all went out as the room shook.

"No!" protested Je Rouge. "No, it can't be! It can't!" He fell on his knees just as the blueish field of light dimmed from around the Matriarch. "It can't be! It can't be," Je Rouge screamed. The light that was once around Amelia was now glowing around Je Rouge. He stood with his eyes turning bright red. His looks became boyish as he stared at Kyle. Then the bluish light faded out. "Yes, I am Simon Chadwick."

Simon was tall, the same height as Je Rouge and still in the same clothes. His hair was long and reddish blond. But he looked as though he was eighteen instead of the mid-forties that Je Rouge appeared to be. He walked toward Amelia and Kyle. "I see you're pretty good at your challenges," he said. "I saw it in you on the playground. I said to myself 'now there is one boy who will be a good challenger.' And I was right."

"Now what? I won, didn't I?" asked Kyle, feeling angry.

"Oh yes, you won, all right," said Simon as he walked closer to Kyle. "You won in finding all ten keys. You won by finding the ingredients and making the potion. You won all the challenges put before you." He picked up his walking stick and pulled out a rapier. "I'm afraid, though, that you forfeit all your winnings and will remain here at Sevenoakes, as one of the collections."

Kyle felt like he was being bullied by Patrick back at the orphanage. "How did I forfeit?"

"You know the secrets of the mansion."

"You mean your secrets," said Kyle.

"Do you think that I could allow you to go out into the world knowing that I killed my family to gain the estate? Or that I'm actually Diabolos Je Rouge? Or that I hold festivals every seven years and keep the losers encased in stone?"

Kyle stood there in silence, feeling another fight was about to erupt.

"And now, young Kyle, you are about to die!" With that, he held the sword pointed at Kyle.

Kyle stood there, glancing to his left and to his right, looking for the sword he brought with him from after killing the suit of armor. Spotting it by the door, he made a leap for it but was stopped by Simon's rapier. "No, no, I can't let you have that," he said.

"Fighting fair?" asked Kyle, sarcastically.

"You want to fight fair, we can," said Simon, "but only on my terms." He allowed Kyle to pick up the sword and laughed when he struggled to raise it over his head. "That will do you no good, young Kyle. You're too tired and weak. That sword is getting heavier in your hands."

Kyle swung the sword at Simon, but Simon stepped out of the way, laughing. The weight of the sword was indeed too heavy for Kyle to make successful use of it. Kyle kept his eye on Simon and tried to raise up the sword.

"I told you to give up back at the pond. I'm sure your bed would feel more comfortable than, say, losing this fight?" said Simon. "Put down the sword and go upstairs to bed."

"No!" yelled Kyle as he took another swing. Simon jumped back, smiling, as the blade fell through the air, missing him completely.

Simon danced over to Kyle and brought down his rapier, cutting Kyle's left arm. This caused Kyle to drop the sword. Kyle looked for another weapon, but like in the basement above, his weapons choices were few.

Amelia leapt forward toward Kyle, but suddenly found herself encased in the light and she couldn't move.

"Kyle, I'm eighteen and in better shape than you. You're weaker, fourteen and have been up all night. Give this up and go to bed," said Simon.

Kyle pulled a torch from one of the support pillars and swung wildly at Simon. Flames flew in the air as Simon jumped back and swatted at the torch. Jumping forward, Kyle shoved the torch at Simon, but Simon dodged the flame and knocked the torch from Kyle's hand. "Good boy, young Kyle, playing with fire!"

Simon swatted at Kyle, backing him against another support pillar. The tip of the rapier cut Kyle's chest above his shirt pocket. Kyle winced in pain and ran from Simon.

Kyle reached the sub-basement door but found it to be locked. "No good, young Kyle. All room doors are locked until after the challenge. You saw that at the pond with the tunnel," shouted Simon.

Kyle continued to look for a weapon but found only small items to throw at Simon. As the rapier sliced through the air, Kyle threw anything he could get his hands on at Simon. "Give it up, young Kyle! I will be the victor over you!" Simon declared.

From deep in the recesses of his mind, Kyle remembered the fight he had with Patrick back at the orphanage. He remembered Timothy and his advice to "know your enemy." Kyle was beginning to know Simon. Simon was good with the rapier but was cheating. Simon cheated at everything. But was he good with fists?

Suddenly, Kyle stopped and looked deep into Simon's red eyes.

Simon, with the rapier raised high, asked, "Giving up so easily?"

"You said this would be a fair fight. Drop your sword and fight me," challenged Kyle.

"Young Kyle, I underestimated you." Simon brought the rapier down by his side. "You really do like pugilism." He smiled then raised up the rapier. "But I don't!" he said, continuing to swat at Kyle.

As with the suit of armor, as with Patrick back at the orphanage, Kyle found his opening and lunged forward, hitting Simon squarely in his nose. Simon grabbed his face and yelled. His eyes grew a brighter shade of red as he stabbed the air in front of Kyle. Kyle dodged each attempt then jumped forward again and hit Simon.

"What are you doing?" asked Simon. "I have the weapon! I have the upper hand!" Simon swung low and hit Kyle in his leg, slicing a four-inch long cut in his thigh.

Kyle fell to the floor then rolled away from Simon just as Simon brought the tip of the rapier down at Kyle. Kyle kicked Simon's leg knocking him off balance. He jumped up and threw himself at Simon, hitting his body and face as many times as he could until Simon fell to the floor. Simon curled up on the floor and started to cry.

At that moment, the light that encased Amelia dimmed and faded away. "Kyle, you did it!" she said.

To Kyle's right, the ten keys burned away leaving the table scarred with ten impressions on its surface. The torches flickered out then back on and soon the room was quiet.

The Matriarch stepped off her pedestal and toward Kyle. "Thank you, Kyle."

"My pleasure," he said as he gazed upon her beauty.

"I have been a statue for over two hundred years. I have witnessed Melvin Everett Horton release everyone one hundred fourteen years ago."

"But if he chose the right key, why were you still a statue?" he asked.

"He chose the correct key to release those trapped in the mansion by Diabolos Je Rouge," she said, "but he didn't beat Diabolos Je Rouge. You did that. All the statues will return to their human form at the age that the spell was cast upon them."

"Even Enov and Gilda?"

"Yes." She looked into Kyles eyes before he turned away. "They were your guide during this Festival. And I know that they were your friends. They will leave and return to their lives as before."

"As before? You mean they'll go back a hundred years ago?" he asked in almost disbelief

"Longer than that, I'm afraid. They were my servants of two hundred years. Now that you released me, they, too shall be released."

"But, what about..."

"Me?" she asked, seeing a building concern in his eyes. "Kyle, I was fourteen when Simon captured me and made into the Matriarch of Time. I have seen many festivals, helped where I could by working with Enov and Gilda, but now that is all gone. I am two-hundred thirty years old, though I was captured at the age of fourteen. I am now back. My life can now continue, at age fourteen."

"But when? Back two hundred years ago?"

"If I choose. But like you, I too, am an orphan. My life can resume back at my time."

Kyle looked around the room then back to the Matriarch.

"Can I come with you, back to your time?"

"That is not possible, Kyle."

"No, it is not!" said Simon, as he stood behind Kyle.

"Simon, I beat you!" said Kyle.

"I was merely taking a rest break," he said, "Now it's time to finish what we've started." He walked past Amelia and pushed her away then took a swing at Kyle. Kyle ducked but threw a punch at Simon's stomach, causing him to bend over.

Simon quickly rose up, holding the rapier in his hand. He swung at Kyle but missed, hitting the bag Kyle used to hold the ingredients for the potion. He turned to see Kyle taking a fighting stance. "I'll have you now, young Kyle," he said as he took a backhanded swing at Kyle.

Kyle stepped back, as the tip of the rapier sliced through the air. He was now up against the wall as Simon stood in front of him. The rapier seemed to hover in the air. Simon brought the tip of the rapier to the wall on one side of Kyle's head, then to the other. He smiled knowing that he had finally beaten the young orphan.

As Simon started his lunge at Kyle, he felt a sharp blow to his back. Simon dropped the rapier an arched his back in pain. He stumbled backward, feeling the pain grow and the blood dripping from the wound. He stopped against a support pillar and looked at Amelia. She stood there with the blood on the sword that Kyle brought with him from defeating the suit of armor.

"You, witch! I kept you young and beautiful all these years! And now, this?" Simon jumped to attack Amelia but felt another blow to his stomach. He looked down and saw the sword buried deep inside of him. He fell to his knees and yelled. His eyes shined the brightest of reds as he looked up and screamed in pain. His feet started to grow solid, as his legs, and his back. He screamed one more time as the bluish light that once encased Amelia now encased him, turning him into stone. The last part of him to die was his red eyes. Soon, they faded into stone, and Simon Chadwick / Diabolos Je Rouge was now and forever, a stone statue, a statue that showed the pain he had inflicted upon everyone he had met.

Kyle looked at the statue then fell to his knees. Exhaustion had finally taken over his body.

"Kyle," said Amelia, "you won. All challenges are over now. We're all free now."

"You saved me," he said, trying to catch his breath.

"And you saved me," she said, brushing the hair out of his eyes. "You saved all of us."

He stood up and looked in her eyes, "Oh Amelia, I'm so tired." He looked at the new cuts on his body inflicted by Simon, then thought for a moment. "But there's one thing. When you return back to your time," he paused to catch his breath, "are you sure that there is no way I can go with you?"

"Kyle, I am from that time and lived to the present as a statue. You were not born then, so you cannot go back. You can only stay here."

Tears came to his eye and he felt them flowing down his cheeks. He thought about losing her and the feelings for her grew stronger. He took her by her shoulders, "Stay with me, here, in this time. I've been thinking of you when I first saw the locket." He looked down, "I'm falling in love with you."

Her face glowed with a radiant smile. "Oh, Kyle, I would love that! And when I saw you struggling through the challenges, I had strong feelings that you would win, and I also had feelings for you, too" But reality hit her. "But how could we survive? Where would we stay?"

"Right here!" came a familiar voice from the door.

"Enov?"

"Yes, my dear!" replied Enov, standing next to Gilda. Both had resumed their natural height of five-foot seven inches tall. "Yes, now that we're free, we can care for thee. Just-"

"Oh, Enov. Enough with the rhymes. Just tell them directly.

"Oh, right, right," he said. "We feel that we can do whatever we want," said Enov. "Therefore, we choose to continue serving you and Kyle."

"Simon Chadwick and Diabolos Je Rouge are gone. We were his first servants and cared for Amelia before she was turned into the statue. Now that Simon and Diabolos are no more, and since we're both still here, you two have a home," assured Gilda.

"And you know what else you won?" asked Enov with a glitter in his eyes. "You won the whole estate, the whole kit and kaboodle!"

"The entire place?" asked Kyle in almost disbelief.

"Yes! And the money, too!" assured Enov.

"When Mister Je Rouge adopted you, you became part of the family. Now that he is gone, you have the entire place, the money, everything," said Gilda.

"Now you two come up out of there and go wash up. Almost time for dinner!" ordered Enov.

"Breakfast, Enov, breakfast," corrected Gilda.

"Oh, oh, yes. Breakfast. Now come up upstairs!"

As he left the sub-basement, Amelia grabbed Kyle's arm. "Kyle, there is one more task for you to perform."

Kyle groaned, "What is it?"

Moments later, they were back in the Ball Room. The floor was surrounded by every statue with Donaldson sitting at the harpsichord. When the music started, each statue returned into human form. Amelia took Kyle by his hands and the two started to dance a slow waltz. The crowd applauded and one by one disappeared, returning to their original time.

When the last person disappeared, the music ended. Donaldson stood from behind the harpsichord and announced, "Master Kyle, Miss Amelia, my service to Sevenoakes is complete. Master Kyle, you have done well during The Festival. For that, I applaud you. For now, I shall go back to my time and leave you two to enjoy your new life."

Kyle looked at Amelia who nodded. "You can stay if you want. I mean, who else is going to get my clothes and tell me when dinner is ready and all that?"

"I would like that, Master Kyle, but I have served this mansion since before Simon, under Lord Elwin, and have amassed my own fortune. I would like to see the world as it was back then."

Kyle looked at Donaldson suspiciously. "You, knew about Simon killing all those people?"

"No, sir. I was sent to France and Spain by Lord Elwin to accompany his staff who were there to expand his business. When I returned six months later, all was done. I was ordered to stay at Sevenoakes by Simon. Soon, Diabolos Je Rouge was employed by Simon to take care of the new business. When Simon died in that tragic accident at sea, I worked for Mister Je Rouge. Now that is over."

"Well, you can still stay. We can even get another butler and you can live here and be waited on."

"Thank you, no," he said. "I do appreciate the offer, but I must decline." He turned to go up the stairs then turned back, "Perhaps someday, I will return." With a smile that looked like the first smile he made over the years, Donaldson disappeared in a flash of blue light, and was gone.

Kyle smiled and looked deeply into Amelia's eyes and slowly moved closer. As they were about to kiss, Enov walked up.

"Breakfast is ready! Now you two come on in here and let's eat!"

In the sub-basement where the flames had long since been extinguished, and Kyle's long nightmare of The Festival had since ended, a statue of Simon Chadwick laid in a crumpled, painful state of shock. The pain on its face bore the fear Simon felt when he realized that his death was upon him at the hand of Amelia. Motionlessly staring up in horror, his tearful eyes started to glow the faintest of red.

THE END

About the Authors

Mack W. Shelton, Jr. found his interest in writing while serving in the U. S. Navy. After serving he developed his skills while in college and eventually becoming the Editor-in-Chief of the college newspaper. His writing include: "Circles of Management," (Publish America-2004)

"Wardenclyffe: The Nikola Tesla Story" screenplay, "Painful Hearts," a short screenplay with Dustin Reed. When he's not working or writing, Mack spends time playing the guitar and bass.

Dustin Reed, co-wrote the short screenplay, "Painful Hearts" with Mack Shelton, Jr. Aside from his regular job he enjoys sports and the company of his two children.

About the Author

Mack W. Shelton, Jr. found his interest in writing while serving in the U. S. Navy. After serving he developed his skills while in college and eventually becoming the Editor-in-Chief of the college newspaper. His writings include: "Circles of Management," (Publish America - 2004), "Wardenclyffe: The Nikola Tesla Story, screenplay, "Painful Hearts" a short screenplay with Dustin Reed. When he's not working or writing, Mack spends time playing the guitar and bass.

Dustin Reed, co-wrote the short screenplay, "Painful Hearts" with Mack Shelton, Jr. Aside from his regular job, he enjoys sports and the company of this children.